Breathe With Me

Breathe with me, toriko...

BRIE'S SUBMISSION

Red Phoenix

Red Phoenix

Edited by Jennifer Blackwell, Proofed by Becki Wyer & Marilyn Cooper
Cover by Shanoff Designs
Formatted by BB eBooks
Phoenix symbol by Nicole Delfs

Dedication

MrRed, thank you for binding me
Heart, body and soul.
I LOVE the call of the jute!

Tono, my muse, thank you for your guidance through
this life.

To the many fans of the gentle Kinbaku Master,
Thank you for your enthusiastic support!
"Breathe with me"
is our shared mantra and joy.

YOU CAN ALSO BUY THE AUDIO BOOK!

Breathe with Me #12

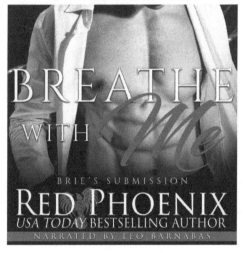

SIGN UP FOR MY NEWSLETTER
HERE FOR THE LATEST RED
PHOENIX UPDATES

FOLLOW ME ON INSTAGRAM
INSTAGRAM.COM/REDPHOENIXAUTHOR

SALES, GIVEAWAYS, NEW RELEAS-
ES, PREORDER LINKS, AND MORE!
SIGN UP HERE
REDPHOENIXAUTHOR.COM/NEWSLETTER-
SIGNUP

CONTENTS

Patience

Tono Nosaka was deeply interested in how the week in Italy would play out after Brie's wedding. Not only did he want to get to know Autumn better while they explored the country together, but he desired to pursue her romantically with Italy as their backdrop.

Her reluctance to be seen in public outside the safety of her friends had almost cost them the trip overseas. It had taken everything in Autumn not to decline when Sir Davis asked her to be a part of Brie's wedding line. If it hadn't been for Lea's presence as the maid of honor, as well as Autumn's own longing to be part of Brie's special day, she would have turned down Sir Davis's request.

Tono had thought it was a real breakthrough when she'd made that commitment, but he'd noticed how nervous she'd been standing in the wedding line with her facial scars fully exposed. Once the reception was under way, she'd started to gravitate toward the shadows, touching her face subconsciously from time to time.

He walked up to Autumn with a glass of wine and stood beside her as she sipped it. "Would you like to dance?"

She shook her head vigorously. "Oh no, you're never getting me out on the dance floor."

"Why not?" he asked with a smirk.

"I may be able to skate with some grace, but I'm hopeless as a dancer with this prosthetic." She banged her hand against it dismissively.

"I'm certain the grace you display on the ice will not be lost in my arms."

She shook her head and grinned. "So *not* going to happen."

Tono decided not to push her. That she hadn't covered her face as soon as the ceremony ended had truly impressed him. She seemed to be slowly growing in confidence, and every step forward was a small triumph that needed to be appreciated.

Autumn watched the couples on the dance floor for a moment and said in a wistful voice, "You know why dogs don't make good dancers? Because they have two left feet." She smiled at him, her eyes sparkling with amusement.

He smiled, but responded by saying, "You look breathtaking tonight."

Autumn chortled. "Stop!"

"It's not polite to turn away a sincere compliment," Tono chided her lightly.

She stared at him for a moment. "I'm sorry, Ren. I just..." Shrugging, she said, "I can't compare to the beauty of Italian women."

He leaned in closer to gaze into her eyes. "You do, and you surpass them."

Autumn laughed as she took a sip of her wine.

Tono noticed Sir Davis motioning to him. He excused himself from her and made his way over.

Sir Davis pulled him aside. "Ren, I know this is a lot to ask, but I've grown tired of the festivities and would prefer to start early celebrations with my wife."

Tono nodded in understanding.

"I've already talked to Brad and he agreed, but I wanted to ask if you mind giving up your dance with Brie?"

"Not at all, Sir Davis. It has been a long day, and I am sure you would like time alone with her."

Sir Davis put his hand on Tono's shoulder. "You are a good friend, Ren Nosaka."

"As are you."

The groom pointed across the courtyard. "I'll need you to tell her to go to that entrance. Warn her that the steps are steep. I don't need my new bride breaking a leg on the way down."

Tono chuckled. "Yes, that would take pleasure and pain to a whole new level."

Sir Davis laughed out loud. "Yes, it would." He was about to walk away when he stopped and turned. Without any explanation, he embraced Tono in a heartfelt hug, slapping him on the back several times before letting go.

Tono watched him walk away and thought, *Love her well…*

He spotted Brie and went over to speak to Master Anderson before joining her. "Mrs. Davis."

"Yes, Tono?"

"Master Anderson regrets that he cannot dance with you tonight, but he asked me to give you this." Tono gave her the small envelope.

Brie took it and smiled, looking around for Master Anderson. When she spied him, she blew Master Anderson a kiss and waved before turning her attention back to Tono.

Her honey-colored eyes drew him in, just as they always had.

"Although the evening is still young, Sir Davis asked me to retrieve you."

"Retrieve me?" she said, giggling.

"Your husband wishes to speak with you—privately."

Brie glanced around, searching for Sir Davis in the crowds. "Where is he?"

"You'll find him down the spiral staircase through there," Tono told her, pointing to an entrance. "I should warn you that the stairs are steep."

He then gave Brie his gift. "I am forsaking my dance so that you may go to him sooner."

Her eyes softened as she gazed into his. "Tono, I would love it if you would dance with Autumn in my stead."

"She is not comfortable on the dance floor."

"Tell her it was my solemn request."

Tono bowed his head slightly and smiled, knowing it was the only thing that might persuade Autumn to consent. "I will tell her."

He turned to leave, but Brie called out his name. "Tono."

"Yes?"

Brie threw her arms around him, pressing her cheek against his chest to listen to his heartbeat. Tono closed his eyes—savoring the moment.

Brie sighed as she pulled away, confessing, "I just needed to hear that."

He looked at her, feeling both love and loss. He kissed her on the forehead and whispered, "May the years ahead be everything you wish for, toriko."

Tono turned away first, letting her go with a full heart.

He walked back to Autumn, who had watched the unusual exchange. "What just happened?"

"I've given my dance away so that the bride and groom can retire for the evening."

"You did?"

"Yes, but Brie asked that you dance with me in her stead."

Autumn shook her head, looking in the direction Brie had disappeared and mumbled, "That little minx."

Tono held his hand out to her with a confident smile. "Will you dance with me, Miss Autumn?"

She blushed deeply but took his hand without further protest, willingly following him onto the dance floor.

He placed his hand on the small of her back and smiled. "Follow my lead."

Once Autumn made a commitment, she gave it all she had. It was something Tono admired about her. At first Autumn was stiff and unsure as she stared down at her artificial leg, trying to move in time with the music.

He stopped and commanded gently, "Look at me."

Autumn glanced up and smiled shyly. Pressing his hand more firmly against her back, he started out slowly, their movements simple but in time with the music.

Her smile widened as she stared into his eyes, and she momentarily forgot where she was. Autumn instinctually moved in sync with him as they made their way around the dance floor.

He leaned down and whispered, "My graceful dancer."

She blushed, fluttering her eyes at him. "Oh Ren…"

Tono stood beside Autumn and watched Sir Davis leave with Brie on their honeymoon the next day. He did not feel the pain of regret, only a desire to move on.

He smiled down at Autumn, proud to have this extraordinary woman by his side. He couldn't wait to explore the wonders of Italy with her.

As he was finishing packing, he looked up and was disheartened to see that she had covered up her face with a veil. "What are you doing, Autumn?"

"I can't face a bunch of strangers with these scars, especially here in Italy where everyone is naturally beautiful."

"But you handled it last night."

"That was different, and believe me it wasn't easy. I did it for Brie, but I made Mr. Davis promise that the pictures would be doctored up so my scars don't ruin their wedding photos."

Tono looked at her in concern. "There was no need for that. You looked stunning last night."

"Ren, I know you can't appreciate where I'm coming from, but I can't tell you how much I hate the questioning stares I get when strangers see my artificial leg. Even worse are the quick glances away when people notice the ugly scars on my face. It's the reason I cover up in public."

He tugged at the material of her veil. "But I need to see your beautiful face. I don't want you to cover up."

She moved away from him. "I'm sorry. I'm not comfortable traveling here any other way."

Tono had been so certain Autumn was slowly coming around, but it seemed she still had a long way to go. "I will only agree if you promise to remove it whenever we're alone."

"Of course, Ren. I feel totally accepted when I'm around you."

Tono thought to himself, *I look forward to the day when my opinion matters more than that of strangers.*

They left Tuscany before noon and headed for Rome for two days to visit the Colosseum, the Forum, and the Vatican. After that, they made their way up the coast to see the Leaning Tower of Pisa, making a quick stop in Siena before ending their trip in Florence.

Autumn was especially excited about visiting the city of Siena after seeing pictures of the tall walls surrounding the classic medieval city. The two of them didn't know until they arrived that their visit coincided with the *Palio della Madonna di Provenzano,* a famous horserace that took

7

place every year.

When Tono had to park far outside the walled city, and saw the sheer number of people going into it, he knew something was up. It wasn't until he entered the walls that he understood a celebration was under way.

The narrow streets of the city were crowded with people cheering enthusiastically as a colorful parade went past.

An Englishman standing beside them took a long, hard look at Autumn with her veil, but couldn't resist spouting off his knowledge as a horse and rider passed. "Each participating *contrade* of this city marches down the streets in all their finery to show off their horse and jockey."

The jockey who passed rode bareback and was dressed in bright colors. Tono appreciated the connection and respect he saw between the animal and its rider.

"Each horse has been blessed by a priest in church. The blokes here take this race very seriously," the man continued.

"That's so fascinating," Autumn exclaimed. "I have to admit, I love all the colors and pageantry."

The Englishman was encouraged by her interest and shared, "There are serious rivalries amongst many of the *contrades*. Some that are centuries old. It makes for a dangerous and exciting race."

Autumn stuck out her hand to shake his. "Before I ask you any more questions, let me properly introduce myself. My name is Autumn Day."

The Englishman laughed.

She grinned. "It's true. My parents thought Autumn

the perfect fit, considering I was born in October."

"They certainly have a sense of humor," he stated, winking at Tono. "Mine is not nearly as entertaining. I'm just simple ol' William Henry."

"So, William, where does the race take place?" Autumn asked, starting back up with her line of questioning.

He smiled smugly when he told her, "In the center of the city itself, at the Piazza del Campo."

Autumn grabbed onto Tono's arm. "Can we go?"

Tono turned to the gentleman. "Are tickets required?"

"Only if you want to sit. Anyone can watch the race, but it's a quick one. Only lasts a little more than a minute."

"All this for a race that lasts only a minute?" Autumn said in awe.

"Twice a year, actually—July and August. The festival for each lasts four days. Tradition means something here," the Englishman replied.

"Truly a rare piece of luck we came today," Tono stated.

"You didn't come for the race?" he asked in surprise.

Autumn giggled from under her veil. "No, it was a happy accident."

The Englishman raised his eyebrows. "Lucky indeed."

Trumpets sounded as another *contrade* came into view. Tono was struck by the pride on the people's faces as they walked past, dressed in their fineries that announced their district. One could feel the connection they had toward their community—and the deep sense of self they gained from it.

It moved him. He felt at home in this place...

When the last of the *contrades* had passed, they followed the crowd as they filtered into the piazza to watch. The center of town had been transformed into a horse track, complete with dirt.

He put his arm around Autumn when the race finally started, impressed by the trust between horse and rider as they careened at breakneck speeds three times around the track. Horses bumped into each other, jockeying for position as the crowd cheered them on.

In a little over a minute the filly with the unicorn as its district symbol surged into first place, barely edging out the brown stallion with a ram as its symbol.

The piazza broke into uproarious applause, the adrenaline of the race still coursing through the entire assembly. Autumn jumped up and down next to Tono, laughing and clapping with delight. If the girl hadn't been wearing that darn veil, he would have kissed her passionately right then and there.

It didn't take long for the piazza to clear out of the spectators, but Tono noticed that for the people of Siena the festivities were just beginning.

"Would you like to stay?" he asked Autumn.

"Oh Ren, I'd love to! I don't think I can get enough of this city. It's like a piece of my heart has been hidden here and I only just found it."

He smiled at her, pleased to hear her express the same feelings he had about the medieval city.

The entire trip Autumn had insisted on separate hotel rooms—even at the castle in Tuscany. She'd told Tono she couldn't handle the thought of him seeing her without the prosthetic leg. No amount of persuading caused her to budge an inch. However, because of their unexpected change of plans in Siena, their only option to stay overnight was a tiny bedroom with a single bed.

They both stared at the miniscule room for several moments before Tono asked, "Are you willing?"

"If it's the only way we can stay the night, then…" Autumn said, sighing nervously. "I guess I am."

Tono thanked the woman who was offering her room for rent. "*Grazie.*"

The woman responded with a smile and gestured them to follow her. "*Vieni a mangiare con noi.*"

Having no idea what the woman was saying, Autumn took Tono's hand with a playful grin and blindly followed her down the hallway. They were led to a dining room where a large wooden table was heavily laden with food. The family was already seated and greeted them with hearty "*Ciaos*".

Tono knew it was their *contrade*, Leocorno, that had won the race, which explained the enthusiastic rejoicing and the continually flowing wine that night. He was feeling the pleasant effects of the fine vino and was anxious to share his kindling passion with Autumn when they finally headed back to the bedroom.

As soon as he shut the door, Tono told her, "Now

that I have you alone, we can do away with this." He ripped the veil from her and held her cheeks in both hands. "I have longed to see your beautiful face all day."

She looked up at him, her eyes reflecting his desire. But the moment he tried to kiss her, Autumn tensed and turned slightly, kissing him demurely on the cheek.

"You're so sweet," she cooed, moving past him to sit on the bed. "I hope you don't mind, but I'll need the lights out before I undress."

Although she had purposely avoided his kiss, the invitation sounded promising. He flicked off the lamp and undressed in the dark before approaching the other side of the tiny bed.

"Even though it's dark, do you mind turning away?"

"Why?" he asked, laughing softly.

"Please?"

Her heartfelt plea could not be ignored, so he turned the other way. It took Autumn a surprisingly long time to ready herself for bed. Before she would allow him to turn, she covered herself under the blankets.

Following suit, he settled under the sheets. Autumn immediately sat up in the bed, placing her hands on either side of her, creating a barrier between them. She giggled nervously. "This is such a small bed. I don't know if either of us will get any sleep."

"I'm not interested in sleep," he said huskily.

She took several deep breaths, obviously trying to quiet her nerves.

"What's wrong, Autumn?"

Giggling lightly, she said, "What do you call a Roman with a cold? Julius Sneezer."

Tono chuckled halfheartedly. "That's funny, but I was being serious."

"Look, Ren, it's been a long, incredibly wonderful day. I feel so lucky to have spent it with you, but my leg is sore and all I really want to do right now is sleep. Can't we talk some other time?"

"Is something wrong?" he asked, now concerned.

"Trust me when I say I just need more time."

Autumn abruptly turned to her side and settled down in the bed.

Tono was stunned. How could this woman who was such a good fit for him in spirit not be responsive to his sexual attraction for her?

Was it a case of not being compatible, or was it something deeper?

Tono slowly lay his head against the pillow, feeling sexually frustrated. Although he was a patient man, he was fully male and had needs of his own.

He thought back to his very first experience with a woman: the one his father had arranged for him. It wasn't until that day he'd understood the perfection that is the female body—both inside and out.

"*Musukosan,* I have a special gift to honor your advancement not only in Kinbaku, but your manhood."

Tono bowed low, surprised by the gesture. His father rarely gave compliments, much less presents. He was a simple man with high standards and did not waste his energy or money on sentimentalities.

"Thank you, *Otosama*." he said with gratitude, feeling overwhelmed.

"You are to return here, fully bathed, in your finest kimono at seven tonight."

Although Tono wondered why he was being instructed to bathe—which seemed an insult—he knew better than to ask why. The respected *bakushi* did not entertain questions. He expected unwavering obedience. As quickly as this gift was given, it could be taken away.

"Yes, *Otosama*."

Tono didn't miss the glint in his father's eyes. When he was almost out the door, his father called out, "Tell her hello for me."

He turned around and bowed again in acknowledgment.

Well, at least he knew it was a woman he would be meeting tonight. Whether it was his father's attempt to entice him into an arranged marriage or he was being asked to perform Kinbaku for an esteemed client was up for debate.

Either way, he would do as he had been asked and meet with the woman, dealing with the consequences later.

Although Tono was against an arranged marriage, and had his father's support, his mother had been adamant that he was to marry at eighteen.

He suspected she desired the marriage for several reasons, not the least of which was the addition of a daughter-in-law his mother could control and lord over. It had his mother salivating for a union.

Tono was not interested in subjecting any young woman to his mother's emotional abuse, which was the main reason he refused to marry. Up to this point, his father had stood behind his controversial decision to remain single.

Had that recently changed?

It was possible that the pressure of tradition and family honor might have proven too much for his father.

To be at odds with his mother was taxing enough, but to openly disobey his *Otosama* would be devastating for them both. It was a battle he did not want to fight.

It was with trepidation that he returned to his father's studio exactly at seven. He entered quietly and was shocked by what he saw when he slid open the door.

Kneeling gracefully in the center of the room was a beautiful geisha.

"Ren Nosakasama?" she called out in a sweet voice.

He nodded as he slid the door closed behind him. So he was to become a man tonight under the skilled hands of a geisha…

Tono was unsure how he felt about that. His father did not understand about love. He'd married the woman arranged for him by his parents at a young age and had done his best to honor that commitment. That was his reality.

To his father, a night with an esteemed geisha would be the ultimate gift a parent could give.

Tono decided in that moment to accept it as such, but it would not have been his personal choice. Despite the example of his father and mother, he was certain a couple could connect on a deeper, more spiritual level during sex. It was his desire to find a partner who complemented both his emotional and physical needs.

The geisha gracefully rocked to her feet and moved over to Tono, gesturing him to follow her into a private room of the studio.

"*Otosama* wished me to express his greeting," he told her as they entered.

She smiled, tilting her head charmingly. "I am honored."

The next few hours were astonishing and remarkable. Fumiko was accomplished in every possible way. She seduced him with her music, playing her instrument for more than an hour at his request. She then treated him to a traditional tea while conversing on a wide variety of topics from politics and philosophy, to art and world travel.

Fumiko was fascinating in her own right, an intelligent woman of many talents. However, she had the ability to build him up in her thoughtful questions and comments so that his young age and lack of experience had no bearing on the conversation.

Tono felt he was her equal, even when it came time to couple with her. He had been afraid he would feel inferior as she guided the lovemaking session. It was quite the opposite.

Fumiko looked at him from across the small table with bedroom eyes and asked, "May I kiss you, Nosakasama?"

"Please call me Ren," he replied with a slight smile. "And yes, Fumiko, you may."

She blushed at being given the honor of calling him

by his first name, and gracefully moved closer to him, resting her hand on his cheek as she leaned forward for a kiss.

The kiss was not aggressive, but she held it for a long time, making the simple contact far more arousing.

Tono felt the rush to his groin and had to adjust his position when she pulled away.

"Would you be more comfortable on the mat?" she suggested.

They both moved over to it and lay down together side by side. Fumiko looked at him but did not make a move. Her painted face exquisite like a painting, but the look in her eye encouraged him to take the lead.

He kissed her again, but with more passion, feeding off the desire she'd carefully built over the evening. When she moaned softly, he felt a deep ache in his loins that demanded attention. Lying back, he opened his kimono, exposing his body to her.

Fumiko smiled at him as she began undoing the red *fundoshi* around his waist. Her eyes lit up when the material fell away and she saw him fully exposed before her.

"You are a distinguished gentleman."

He gave her a smirk, which quickly disappeared when she wrapped her red lips around his hard cock. Tono groaned and she met his groan with moans of her own as she licked, sucked and teased his shaft.

With subtle movements, she pulled at her own kimono, exposing her shoulder and allowing the barest peek of her breast. Although he had seen numerous women naked in his years practicing Kinbaku in the studio, it drove him wild to catch stolen glimpses of her nipple.

When he couldn't take it any longer, he reached out to caress her breast. Fumiko pressed herself against his hand, letting him know she enjoyed his touch. He pulled down on the silk, wanting to see more of her naked skin as she sucked him.

She stopped momentarily, holding his cock in her hand, and gave him a seductive smile. Tono shook his head, taken by her beauty, but he soon threw back his head groaning in pure ecstasy.

Fumiko was exceptionally skilled with her mouth.

Tono would have come if she hadn't stopped. She stood up and untied the belt of her kimono, letting the silk fall to the floor, exposing her perfect body to him.

"You are breathtaking," Tono stated in awe.

She smiled, somehow keeping a virtuous demeanor even though she was standing completely naked before him.

"Come to me," he commanded, needing to touch her.

Fumiko moved with grace as she lay down, looking up at him with eyes that were innocent yet expectant. "I am yours to explore."

Tono smiled to himself as he ran his hand over her smooth skin, wanting to touch every part of her body. In his Kinbaku sessions, he had inadvertently touched his models in intimate places as he bound them, but he had never been given the opportunity to freely explore the female form. He took his time, touching, licking and kissing every part of Fumiko, from her small toes, the sensitive backs of her knees, those sexy indents of her lower back, to the luscious curve of her breasts. Nothing went overlooked as he reveled in every part of her body.

She responded passionately to his caresses, moaning in his ear. The girl was wet, making him groan with excitement, his cock aching to know her hidden beauty.

"I want you, Ren," she said, looking at him almost bashfully, which only made him desire her all the more.

Tono positioned himself between her legs and stared at her ruby-red pussy framed in dark pubic hair. For a moment he panicked, overcome by the fear of looking like an idiot before this beautiful woman as he tried to make love to her—but those fears were totally unfounded.

Fumiko was an artisan of lovemaking, and Tono was far from her first virgin. Rather than instructing him verbally and highlighting his lack of knowledge, she moved in such a way as to encourage his dominance over her while maintaining subtle control.

He groaned in pleasure as she took hold of his shaft and rubbed it against her slippery clit, using his shaft for her pleasure and driving him crazy because of it.

When the drive to fuck her became too much, Tono gazed into her eyes. She positioned his cock against her wet opening and threw her head back, crying, "I need you, Ren."

He plowed into her depths, and for a moment he couldn't breathe. The silky warmth of her inner embrace was beyond anything he'd imagined.

Tono had to struggle for control, his body already priming itself for an orgasm.

Fumiko understood his battle, and pulled lightly on his balls, distracting him from his release. He closed his eyes for a moment and slowed his breathing, not wanting this incredible feeling to end so quickly.

When he opened them again, he kept his cock still as he leaned down to kiss her. "You are so beautiful, Fumiko," he said in a raspy voice tinged with lust.

She kissed him back, her big dark eyes communicating her passion and need for him.

"I don't think I can last..." he confessed as he stroked her pussy several times and felt the impending orgasm begin to build again.

"You are not supposed to, Ren. Enjoy the feeling."

He threw back his head and grunted gutturally as he shot load after load of his essence into her divine body. He'd never known he could come like that. Afterward, he collapsed on top of her, his heart racing from the intensity of his climax.

Fumiko ran her fingers through his hair. "You are such a handsome and accomplished man. I'm truly honored to be your first."

He lay silent in her embrace, his mind completely blown by the experience. Truly, heaven lay between her legs, and he longed for another taste.

Tono looked up, sweat running down his forehead. "You inspire me to try again." He glanced down at his cock, already growing hard at the thought.

Would he ever get enough of her?

Suddenly there was a commotion outside. Before he could react, the door to the room quickly slid open. Tono shielded Fumiko's naked body with his own as he faced the intruder.

"How dare you!" his mother screamed. "You have disgraced the family!"

Tono glared at her, saying nothing.

Even this extraordinary moment she had to steal from him...

"Out!" he yelled.

She hesitated for a moment, then turned in a huff, sliding the door hard behind her.

Tono looked down at Fumiko. "I'm so sorry."

She caressed his jaw. "No, Ren, it is I who is sorry for you."

Tono lifted himself off her small frame. He picked up her silken kimono, handing it to Fumiko, before grabbing his *fundoshi*. He tied it on with overly tight knots, trying to calm down the fury raging in his heart.

His mother had done this not only to humiliate him in front of the respected geisha, but to steal this rite of passage from her son.

Tono shook his head, remembering the pain of that moment, realizing his mother had no respect for him as a man.

There had been only one way out from under the heavy weight of her oppression. But the price—it had cost him nearly everything.

He looked over at Autumn's sleeping form, huddled under the covers, and smiled to himself. Here was a woman who had an amiable spirit that was in sync with his own. Although he desired to explore a more physical relationship with her while in the romantic ambiance of Italy, he had continually been met with gentle but unyielding resistance the entire time here.

Tono thought he understood her reasons and did not push her limits the remainder of the trip, satisfying himself with the pecks on the cheek and hand-holding she was inclined to give him.

However, that would all change once they were back in Denver. It was time to challenge Autumn and find out if he could break through the impenetrable fortress she'd built around herself.

To the world she was a fun-loving spirit, courageously living her life despite her disability. Many were unaware she was also a talented ice-skater.

Tono, however, saw beneath those truths everyone else could see. Hidden deep inside Autumn was a woman who longed to be loved, not just for her personality and grit, but for her raw femininity. It was something she would not admit, even to herself, but he sensed it.

The call of her sexual being cried out to him, begging to be freed.

Rare Flower

Tono had been surprised when Master Anderson requested Tono meet with him at his home immediately upon returning to the States with Autumn.

He made the long drive up to the suburb set in a quiet valley nestled in the foothills of the Rockies. The view of Denver once Tono got there was spectacular. He understood perfectly why Master Anderson had chosen this home and why he now found it so hard to leave.

"Nosaka, I'm sorry about the short notice, but I'm running out of time and can't waste another second."

Tono naturally assumed he was being asked to help pack. "Although I'm still healing from the surgery, I'll help however I can."

Master Anderson laughed. "No, no... I don't need help moving, Nosaka. You need to heal, man. What I'm asking is for you to look after my place."

"Ah... I see," Tono said, taken aback by the request. "For how long?"

Master Anderson grinned. "Let me back up and try that again. I would like you to be the caretaker of this home for as long as you want the position." He looked around his newly built range-style home and pointed outside with a worried expression on his face. "I spent too much time designing this place and creating a garden to complement it. How can I abandon my baby now?"

Tono looked out at the fenced area, lined with flourishing native vegetation and accented with the lone pole in the center of the yard. He understood how flora could become dear to a person—similar to extended family—when a person harbored a nurturing spirit like Master Anderson.

It was a quality about the humorous Dom few seemed to recognize.

"It *would* be a shame to see the garden neglected," Tono agreed.

"Exactly!"

"However, I'm not in the position to rent such a large home."

Master Anderson chuckled. "I'm really mucking this up. Look, I need you to care for this house and the garden. I put way too much of myself into this place to let renters have at her. Then there's my Academy. I need someone nearby looking after my interests."

"But you have Ms. Clark staying behind, don't you?"

"I do, but I want someone outside the inner workings of the Academy to be responsible for watching over it in my stead. Someone with an objective eye and a commanding, yet agreeable, spirit."

Tono smirked, knowing that Ms. Clark was not an easy woman to work with. He had his own misgivings about the Domme, based on her treatment of Brie during training. "I can appreciate that," he replied evenly.

"So in essence, by staying here you would provide me with peace of mind while maintaining the upkeep of my investments." Seeing that Tono was still not convinced, Master Anderson added, "I was told you sold off most of your furniture when you left for Japan. Well, my furniture isn't being used. Anything you don't care for can go into storage. A win/win, wouldn't you agree?"

"That doesn't seem like a fair exchange," Tono scoffed. "It feels like charity."

Master Anderson put his hand on Tono's shoulder. "It's true, and I'm not above begging. I'm under a considerable amount of stress right now. You have no idea how much I would pay to relieve some of it. By accepting my offer, you would be doing me a huge favor. If you want to consider that charity, then I'm asking you to give generously."

Tono laughed. "You are an odd man."

"Nosaka, I'm being completely on the up and up here. I want you to take care of my property. If you won't do it, I'll have to pay someone who will. It's as simple as that. However, I would prefer it to be someone I personally know and trust."

With that argument, Master Anderson had broken down the last of his resistance. "Fine, I will care for your home and keep watch over the Academy for you."

"You're a good egg, Nosaka."

Tono laughed at the compliment. "Coming from you, I'm sure that is meant as a positive statement. Coming from Sir Davis or Marquis Gray, it would be a clear insult."

Master Anderson burst out in a low laughter. "Oh, young Brie and her egg fiasco... I'll never forget it. Poor Thane."

"Poor Marquis Gray," Tono interjected. "He was forced to sample them all."

The two Doms chuckled, reflecting on Brie's failed cooking attempts at the Training Center.

"I'll be honest, Nosaka. There was no way I was allowing anything cooked by her hands at the party she attended with me that night after the omelet incident," Master Anderson told him. "She may be a talented individual in many areas, but cooking isn't one of them."

"At that point you were wise to do so. However, Brie has tackled that shortcoming since."

"True, I've heard that from Thane. He's not one to sugarcoat things, so when he tells me that she makes a mean Ribollita, I have to take his word for it."

"I respect her tenacity," Tono said. "She isn't one to sit idly by when she knows there's an area that needs improvement."

"No, she's not, and neither is Thane. They do make a good complement for each other."

Tono nodded his agreement.

"So what are your plans in Denver?" Master Anderson asked.

"I believe the Rocky Mountains will be a perfect canvas for my art. Although I am still recuperating and cannot do suspension yet, I plan to photograph my subs in rope using the natural environment here as the backdrop."

"That would be stunning, Nosaka. Mind sending me

pics of some of your shots? I know I will miss the mountains here," he added wistfully, staring out the window at the snowy peaks towering above.

Tono glanced at the backyard thoughtfully. "But I believe I will start here. The fence will give me the privacy I'll need, and your native foliage will frame my subs well when I do simple ties that do not require lifting."

Master Anderson put his right hand on his chest. "It would do my heart good to know my plants will have a place in your art."

Tono smiled humbly.

Master Anderson stuck out his hand. "So, do we have a deal?"

Tono took his extended hand and shook it firmly. "Yes, I will care for your interests to the best of my ability."

"Hallelujah!" Master Anderson exclaimed. "One more thing I can check off the list."

"When would you like me to move in?"

"Believe it or not, I'm out of here in five days."

Tono shook his head in amazement.

"I told you, man, you really are doing me a favor."

"I still maintain I'm getting the better end of the deal."

"Oh…" Master Anderson said, looking concerned. "I forgot to mention Courtney."

"Who's Courtney?"

"Never mind, I'll take care of it," Master Anderson assured him.

"Take care of what exactly?"

The man grinned, shaking his head. "Forget I said anything."

Although Tono had his reservations, the offer was too good to pass up. He'd lived with Autumn since the surgery, and it was time he moved into his own place so that he could court her properly.

Tono watched Autumn with concern as she struggled to carry in the last box of his stuff. When he tried to assist her, she rebuffed him. "Stop right there, Ren. You know you aren't supposed to lift anything heavy," she chided, placing the box on the floor and putting her hands to her hips. "You have to promise that you won't overdo it unpacking all this stuff by yourself."

He knew and respected the limits of his body. Injuring himself and thereby slowing his recovery was not an option. He'd lost valuable time after the death of his father and was unwilling to lose any more. "I promise not to undo all the hard work you put into helping me move here."

"Good, because I would have to punish you if you did."

Tono raised an eyebrow. "Punish me?"

A blush crept over Autumn's cheeks. "Not like that. Oh lord…" She looked around nervously, suddenly blurting, "Whoever said an acorn doesn't fall far from the tree never saw an oak tree growing beside a cliff."

Tono shook his head, a grin playing on his lips as he

came up to her and guided Autumn to a kitchen chair. He knelt down beside her and began gently massaging her leg, knowing that the prosthetic must be causing her great discomfort with all the lifting she'd done that day.

Autumn quietly moaned in pleasure, relaxing in the chair as she let his fingers work their magic. "How did you know?"

"I saw the pain in your eyes."

She stared at him in wonder. "You notice many things, Ren."

He chuckled lightly, shrugging. "Not any more than most."

"No, I've never met anyone like you."

"What would you say if we took this off?" he asked casually, pointing to her prosthetic.

Autumn stiffened and sat up straight, shaking her head. "No, I can't."

Tono touched her protesting lips with his index finger. "Yes, you can. How else can I properly massage the area?"

"No, you don't understand."

"But I do," he told her smoothly as his hands drifted down to the pin that held her prosthetic in place. "There is no reason for you to fear me."

She put her hand on his wrist to stop him. "Please don't. I can't. Not with you."

He looked up at her. "You spent how many weeks looking after my needs. Why won't you trust me to care for yours now?"

It took his words a moment to sink in as he gazed into Autumn's green eyes. He could see the fear—the fear of rejection she was trying so desperately to hide from him.

"Trust me," he ordered gently.

Autumn took a deep breath and let go of his wrist, her entire body trembling as he pressed against the pin, releasing its hold. He removed the prosthetic and then began unrolling the liner beneath it with gentle hands.

She held her breath as it slipped off, turning her head as the stump of her leg was exposed to him.

Tono suspected it was to avoid the expression on his face when he saw it for the first time, so he commanded, "Look at me."

She turned back to him slowly, her brows furrowed in concern.

He ran his hand reverently over the scars on the end of her stump. "Truly, it's remarkable the healing power of the body, isn't it?"

She said nothing, still quivering under his touch.

Tono concentrated on bringing relief to the raw areas while manipulating the overtaxed muscles of her upper thigh. "You overdid it today. In trying to spare me, you hurt yourself."

Autumn shook her head, snorting lightly. "I've been through far worse, Ren. This was nothing—trust me."

He continued to caress her skin as he hummed a favorite country tune of his, letting the intimacy of the moment linger between them. He felt a connection with Autumn on a soul level. It was not the same bond he'd felt with Brie, but...it was equally compelling.

"I find your body fascinating, Autumn," he stated as he massaged her. "It's so incredibly strong and yet still feminine and delicate. The grace that you display on the ice is as inspiring as it is beautiful."

She slapped her leg as if it were an inanimate object. "There's nothing pretty about it, but it does the job well enough."

Tono refused to allow her to dismiss his compliment. Taking her hand, he guided it back to her leg. "Respect the beauty of this instrument."

A tear formed in her eye as she grazed the raised skin of her thick scars. "I don't find it beautiful," she whispered to him.

"But it is…" he insisted.

Tono was finding Autumn a much harder conquest than any he'd ever encountered before. She had multiple facets to her personality.

On one side she was inspiring and friendly. The kind of person you couldn't help but admire, yet still felt completely at ease with. Another side of her was kindhearted and shy, wanting to help those in need, but preferring to hide in the shadows.

Then there was the unique side, which was both funny but hard like granite. That fighting spirit that had helped her triumph despite her physical setbacks also protected her from ever opening up to another—her simple jokes providing an easy escape whenever fear set in.

The woman was fascinating and beautiful in both body and spirit. Extremely rare like the Rothschild's orchid, and apparently as difficult to possess.

Haunting Dream

Tono was walking in the Japanese city park, Shinjuku Gyoen, admiring the breathtaking scenery. It was the peak of the cherry blossoms season, and their sweet fragrance permeated the air, lifting his spirits. He felt alive in the deepest sense of the word, connected with everything and everyone around him.

He began walking over the arched bridge on his way to the small isle with the ancient tree that dominated the area, but he took a moment to stop midway, looking down into the water. Koi swam about, their gold color contrasting beautifully against the greenery and pink blossoms above.

Truly a magical place...

He felt at home here, a part of nature and in harmony with the living things around him. It seemed only natural that he should see Brie standing under the protective branches of the timeless tree. He waved, glad to share this moment with her.

But she ignored him as if he weren't there.

Tono beckoned Brie over to him. She just stared

ahead and then turned away, disappearing behind the immense trunk of the tree.

Fear struck at his heart.

Tono walked briskly, an ominous feeling creeping over him when he heard her desperate sobs. With trepidation, he rounded the massive trunk and found her on the ground, her head buried in her arms as she leaned against the tree.

"What's wrong, Brie?"

When she didn't respond, he knelt down and touched her.

"Toriko…"

She looked up at him, her eyes black like the never-ending night with tears that would not stop.

"What's happened? What's wrong?"

Brie didn't speak, but she looked up into his eyes and shared her darkness with him.

Tono couldn't breathe as hopelessness and fear washed over him.

"Fight it!" he commanded, not just to her but to himself, knowing they were both about to be consumed in the inky gloom.

Brie broke eye contact and buried her head in her arms again.

He felt his breath come back, life returning to his soul.

She said nothing, fighting the darkness alone.

Tono reached out to her and was horrified at how cold she felt—like the dead.

"Toriko, I will share your darkness with you. We'll enter it and fight or die together trying."

She remained still, ravaged by it.

When Tono tried to pull her up so he could hold her, Brie became like stone—heavy and unpliable. He was unsuccessful in his attempts and cried out, understanding the gravity of the situation.

"Toriko, you must let me in. You cannot fight this alone."

When Brie looked up again, all life seemed to have drained from her face, her gaze now a dark void that paralyzed him.

Brie stood up slowly, her eyes now focused ahead as she started toward the water.

There was nothing he could do as she entered the lake and, step by step, submerged herself until she disappeared under the watery depths.

As if released from invisible bonds, Tono suddenly found he could move again. He ran to the water and dived in, reaching out wildly until he found her under the dark waters.

Tono carried her lifeless body back onto the shore, and screamed up at the sky in agony.

His cry echoed through the air as the cherry blossoms began to fall like snow around him, covering everything—the ground, the water, and her body—with dying blossoms.

Tono woke up, his heart pounding painfully in his chest. He'd never had a dream so vivid or horrific.

It wasn't even a question for him as he picked up the phone. He needed to hear Brie's voice and confirm she was okay no matter where she was or what she was doing. The idea that he had just witnessed her death was too terrible to contemplate.

To his relief, Brie immediately picked up.

"Is everything okay, Brie?"

Her laughter was light on the other end. "Yes, everything is wonderful here! We made it back home just a few days ago."

"Oh…" Tono couldn't reconcile the dream he'd just endured and the joy he heard in her voice now. "I am relieved to hear it."

She would never know how much…

"I had a dream that was disturbing," he explained, keeping it simple. "In it you were crying."

"Well, I have been crying," she admitted gleefully. "However, they have been happy tears."

Tono expelled a long, drawn-out sigh. "Hearing the joy in your voice relieves me greatly." He wiped the tears that had formed in his eyes and commanded himself to breathe again.

Brie was fine. Whatever that dream was about, she was alive and thriving.

It came as a surprise to him when Brie shared that she was pregnant. Because of their uncommon bond, she'd naturally assumed that Tono had dreamed about the happy event and was calling her about it.

He did not correct her, unwilling to mar her joy with his nightmare.

Brie peppered him with questions, but he only half-listened, his mind preoccupied with the visions that lingered. But when she asked about Autumn, he found himself suddenly smiling.

"She is well, too."

"That's all you're going to give me?"

"We are comfortable together."

Brie's joyous laughter fortified his heart.

"Well, knowing you, that speaks volumes," she stated.

"So you are good?" he asked, needing that assurance.

"I am, Tono." At the end of the call, she added, "Thanks for checking up on me. I appreciate that you cared enough to call."

Tono hung up the phone, feeing relieved but still disquieted in his spirit.

It was possible the dream had no significance, but the image of her walking into the lake would remain with him forever.

The dream inspired Tono to pursue Autumn with more resolve. Life was unpredictable, and he was unwilling to let this woman slip through his fingers because of her fears.

"Autumn, I would like you to meet me at my new place. I'm cooking pizza, and you're free to bring whatever you want to add to the meal."

"That sounds like fun, Ren."

Tono readied the great room, covering it in red candles, the color of luck. He then went to the drawer in his bedroom and got out the *omamori* he'd gotten from the Itsukushima Shrine. It had the image of a deer on it and was a talisman for finding his life partner. He was certain Autumn was the one; he just needed to convince her of it. He propped it up on the mantel of the great room with reverence.

Autumn arrived ahead of schedule with a Caesar salad, garlic bread, and a local craft beer in her hands.

He took the items from her, complimenting, "We shall be feasting tonight."

She looked around the large space, touched by all the lit candles and simple furniture that made up the room now. "It's beautiful, Ren. You've really transformed this place to reflect you."

"Thanks, you were part of my inspiration."

She blushed and moved toward the aromas wafting from the kitchen. "It smells heavenly."

"It should, I used your recipe."

She giggled. "Although it seems I was trying to compliment myself, I'm honored. It smells like you did a fine job."

He walked behind her and put an arm around Autumn's shoulders. Not too intimate, but definitely a possessive hold. He felt her momentarily stiffen in his arms, but she relaxed when he made no other move.

"I learned from the best," he said in a low, seductive tone, squeezing her tighter before letting go.

Autumn turned to face him. "A mushroom walks into a bar, and the bartender says, 'Hey, you can't drink here.' Mushroom says, 'Why not, I'm a Fun-gi!'"

He chuckled, moving in closer. "Do you always make jokes when you're nervous?"

"No... I..." Her lips curled into a smile. "I suppose I might."

"Why are you nervous with me?"

Autumn shrugged and scooted past him. "Why don't we have a beer?"

"Would it help with your nerves?"

She held up two bottles. "It might."

"Then, by all means, let's have a beer."

Tono took them from her and popped the bottle caps off and handed one back. Autumn clinked her bottle against his. "Here's to good pizza and good friends."

"And a little bondage," Tono added, putting the bottle to his lips with a grin.

She froze for a moment. "Are you..."

He nodded. "Yes, I plan to introduce you to my jute tonight."

He saw that momentary flash of fear but, to her credit, Autumn pushed through it and asked, "What kind of rope work?"

"Something simple. A gentle introduction."

He was relieved when she smiled. "I like the sound of that."

The timer went off for the pizza. Grabbing his mitt, Tono pulled the pie, covered in bubbling cheese, out of the oven. "First, we dine on the patio." He smiled gave her a flirtatious smile, adding, "And then I tie you up."

Her giggle was a little higher pitched than normal, hinting that Autumn was feeling anxious, but the excitement in her eyes let Tono know she desired to connect with him in this way.

Progress.

Tono took his time eating the simple meal, chewing each bite slowly as he watched her. He purposely drew out the time before their first scene, wanting to heighten the experience for Autumn.

When he determined the time was right, Tono stood up and held out his hand to her. "Come with me, beautiful. Let's find out how you respond to my jute."

He noticed the increase in her breathing and smiled to himself as he led her inside. "Go to the guest room and dress in the silk robe." When she looked like she was about to protest, he added, "Trust me, the only binding I want you to feel is my jute, not your street clothes."

"But I can keep my underclothes on, right?"

He shrugged with a slight smile. "I leave that totally up to you."

Tono washed and dried his hands before going to the stereo and turning on his favorite flute music. The soothing sound of the instrument filled the great room as he went to his bedroom to change into his black kimono.

He returned and stood on the mat with jute in hand, waiting for Autumn to make her entrance.

When he heard the door of the guest room finally open, he walked down the hallway to meet her.

Her eyes lit up when she saw him. "Oh, Ren, you look so handsome."

"Thank you. You're equally as handsome," he said with a playful grin.

She turned her head toward the music. "It's a lovely

melody."

"It's the music of Native American flautist Carlos Nakai. He is my favorite artist. He blends his music with other cultures, including that of Japan. I had the honor of meeting him a few years ago. He's as soulful in person as he is when he plays his handcrafted flutes."

"If this song is an indication of his work, I think he just became a favorite of mine as well."

Tono guided her back into the great room and noticed when she looked up at him her expression held both desire and apprehension.

"There is no reason to be afraid, Autumn. Everything I do tonight will be for your pleasure."

She gave him a hesitant smile. "I trust you, Ren. I just feel this is a pivotal moment between us. What if I don't like it?"

"Then we will stop."

"Okay…" Autumn took a deep breath. "I think you should know that of all the people I have ever met, you are the only one I would trust to do this."

"It's my hope that you not only enjoy the experience, but that it moves you on a deeper level."

She put her hand in his. "Lead the way, Tono Nosaka."

It was the first time she had called him by his title, and it stirred the Dominant in him.

"Sit on the mat," Tono instructed, holding out his hand to help her to the ground, knowing her prosthetic made it more difficult. Once Autumn was settled, he positioned himself behind her and put the rope on the floor next to him.

"I need to wrap my arms around you."

Nervous giggles met his words. "Okay."

With permission given, Tono put one arm around her chest above her breasts and the other beneath them. She tensed at this more intimate contact, so he held her tighter and whispered, "I want you to match your breath with mine."

She nodded, and within a few moments, he felt her relax in his arms.

Tono picked up the jute and instructed, "Hold out your hands and feel the rope that is about to bind you."

She took it and ran her fingers over it. "I expected to it to be softer."

"The jute must be strong enough to suspend a person." He leaned over her shoulder and rubbed the cord between his fingers. "It has been conditioned so that it is gentle on the skin, but still leaves an attractive mark."

Autumn shivered in his arms.

It was time to see if she responded to the call of his rope.

Tono halved the length of the jute and started at the top of her chest where his arm had just been. He was careful as he bound her, making sure not to touch her breasts although he purposely came close. He took his time, letting the jute slide against her skin, grazing the intimate areas he would not touch with his hands. He noticed the effect it had on her as the barest outline of her nipples showed underneath her silk robe.

He hoped to convince her to lose the bra and panties next time—provided there was a next time.

Tono began tightening the rope around her torso.

"Do you want it tighter or is this comfortable?"

"Tighter," she told him.

Another good sign...

He tightened it slightly, keeping in mind that this was her first experience. Some novices asked for more and then suddenly panicked.

"Does this feel good?"

"No, tighter please, Tono."

His loins surged with pleasure, hearing that title spoken so freely from her lips.

"Do not forget to match my breath. If it becomes overwhelming, say so."

She nodded, closing her eyes to concentrate on his breathing. He tightened the rope even further and then began the next set of knots. When he was done, he placed his hands on her shoulders and closed his eyes, taking in this unique moment of intimacy.

Her spirit was like the yellow light of the sun, and he basked in it for several minutes before standing up.

Tono picked up his camera and explained, "I would like to take a picture of you bound in my rope."

For the first time, real panic showed on her face. "Oh no, Ren, please don't!" she whimpered, struggling in her bonds as she tried to cover her face with her hair.

He put the camera down and called out to her. "It's okay, Autumn. I won't take a picture."

She looked up at him like a frightened animal. "Please don't ever take a picture of me, especially when my face is not covered up."

He knelt beside her, cradling her cheek in his hand. "There is no need to cover up and no need to shy away from my camera. Every part of this face is pleasing."

A lone tear ran down her cheek. "Please, Ren, untie me."

Tono was surprised by the turn of events, but he now better understood how deeply she feared her own body.

Only love and patience could combat that.

He went to the stereo and switched the song to one that was slow and light, like a whisper on the wind. He then sat behind her, determined to continue their intimate connection even as he unbound her from the rope.

"Close your eyes, and listen to the music as the jute releases its hold. The untying is as spiritually significant as the binding."

She nodded, but he could feel her thoughts were not with him.

"Breathe with me…" he whispered in her ear.

Almost immediately, she was in sync with him again. He was slow and meticulous as he loosened her from the jute. As he undid the knots, he told her, "I admire the classic lines of your face. You are truly breathtaking." He chuckled, remembering their first meeting. "I couldn't take my eyes off you the first time we met. I could tell you that I don't see the scars on your face, but that would be untrue. I see them, Autumn, and they are as beautiful to me as the rest of you."

She shook her head.

"It's true. They are a part of you as much as your dark auburn hair and those mesmerizing green eyes. I would not wish them away. They speak to your strength and only enhance your allure."

He let the rope fall to the ground and enfolded his arms around her.

Tono felt the wetness of her tears and understood she was struggling with his words. Hopefully they would find a home in her heart. A seed planted that would slowly begin to grow and flourish…

Tono turned her bodily toward him so he could gaze into her eyes. "You are beautiful, Autumn Day."

She glanced down at her lap, saying nothing, with a slight smile on her lips.

Tono suddenly felt unsettled, Brie flashing to his mind. He brushed off the vision, afraid he might be suffering from old feelings he'd kept buried and that were only now resurfacing.

"What's wrong, Ren?"

He shook his head, rubbing his chest. "Nothing a kiss can't cure."

She blushed but pursed her lips obligingly, ready to give him a peck.

"No, Autumn," he said, leaning in closer. "I want to kiss you like a man should. Your lips have been calling to me for weeks. I can no longer deny them."

Her eyes widened in alarm. "Oh Ren…I'm not—"

"Shhh…" he said, not taking no for an answer this time. Tono cradled her neck in his hand as he moved in for the kiss. At first her lips were hard and unyielding, but little by little they softened against his.

Flicking his tongue across them, he held her firm when Autumn attempted to pull away. Victory was finally his when she parted her lips and he tasted her mouth for the first time.

Autumn's moan was low and sultry, causing his shaft to harden. He kissed her more deeply then, running his tongue over her teeth before thrusting deeper. Autumn's breath came in short gasps, her body tensing against him.

Tono broke the kiss and looked into her eyes. He saw obvious fear and the glimmer of raw desire.

He released the light hold he had on her neck and leaned back.

Autumn stared at him, looking like she was ready to flee.

"Is it wrong for me to want you?" he asked.

She shuddered, taken aback by the frank question. "I'm not ready for this, and why would you want to?"

"You are ready, but you're allowing fear to control you."

She sounded insulted when she answered. "I'm a fighter. Nothing controls me."

"Then explain your question about why I would want to."

Autumn threw her hands up. "Ren, you can have any girl you want, as many as you want, and with the skills you require. Why—what possible reason—would you choose me?"

"I'm incredibly attracted to you."

"But why?" she cried, her claws suddenly coming out as if he had said something offensive. "Do you have some weird amputee fetish, or do you just feel sorry for this little crippled skater?"

Tono was surprised by the accusation. but only smiled as he took her hand which had balled into a fist of anger during her outburst. He held her wrist firmly as he slowly opened her fist, exposing her tender palm. He kissed the center of it as he looked at her and repeated, "I'm attracted to you, Autumn."

"Why, Ren? I need to know," she pleaded.

Now that he had Autumn's attention, he told her the truth. "I am fascinated by those bright green eyes that sparkle with hidden secrets I want to know." His eyes drifted down to her lips. "And I am entranced by the sensual curve of your mouth—the way it teases me with those arched lips that smile so freely." Tono boldly stared at her chest. "And your body begs for me to touch it, to discover its many pleasures."

He gazed into her soulful eyes again. "I am completely captivated, and it is only because of my self-control and respect for you that I do not push you to the floor and let my passions run wild."

She sounded shocked. "I had no idea you fel—"

"You may not acknowledge my desire for you, but it is very real. I have been patient long enough..."

"What are you saying?"

"I want to move forward in this relationship. I'm tired of standing on the sidelines waiting for you to invite me in."

Autumn stared at him, not saying a word.

He let the silence extend, allowing her thoughts to play out without interruption.

"You frighten me, Ren."

"In what way?"

"I don't know, and that's what scares me."

He tilted his head. "Did you enjoy kissing me?"

She unconsciously touched her lips with her fingers, shaking her head slowly. "No, it's too much."

"Too much?"

"I told you I wasn't ready."

"But your body is. I felt the way you responded. Why can't you let go of your inhibitions and give in to your desires?"

She sighed heavily, looking bereft. "We work so well together as friends. Why do you want to ruin it?"

"I want more." He saw her tremble, his statement having more of an effect than she wanted to admit.

"What if I don't?"

"We will remain friends, of course, but I would be forced to move on. Although I am a patient man, I am still a man with sexual needs."

"Couldn't you just use one of the subs for release?"

He looked at her with a pained expression. "I'm looking for more than that, Autumn."

"But what if I can't be what you need?"

"How will we know unless we try?"

She let out a small gasp. "I'm so afraid of losing our friendship. I don't think you can appreciate how precious it is to me."

"I can, because I feel the same way."

"Then why mess with it?" she pleaded.

"I cannot continue to stand in stagnant water. It has no life force."

Autumn closed her eyes. "I don't want to lose you, Ren."

He lifted her chin with his finger. "Then let me in…"

Autumn drove home soon after, explaining that she needed time to think about what he'd said. Tono let her go, not interested in exploring the relationship further unless she was all in.

Autumn had to want this as much as he did, or it would end in heartache for them both.

It wasn't until he was outside, sitting on his mat on the backyard patio, that he felt that unsettling sensation again. He touched his chest, now more aware of the pain.

Tono realized it hadn't been his growing feelings for Autumn that caused it.

He immediately got up and returned to the house, picking up his phone and dialing Brie's number. It went straight to voicemail. He couldn't explain why, but the ominous feeling he'd experienced in the dream returned full force.

He left a message. "Brie, I need to know you are okay. I realize we just spoke yesterday, but I need to hear your voice."

He placed the phone on the nightstand beside his bed and tried to rest, but sleep proved impossible as the image of Brie disappearing under the water haunted his thoughts.

Tono was relieved when the phone finally rang and he saw that it was her number. "Brie?"

"No, Tono Nosaka. This is Candy. I got your message for Brie and she gave me permission to let you know Sir Davis was involved in a plane crash last night. She is fine and Sir is alive but in critical condition. That's all I can tell you right now because we're waiting on the doctor for more information. Brie doesn't want anyone else to know until she's had a chance to speak with the medical team."

"I will not share the news, but please let her know I'm here if she needs me."

"I will."

"Thank you."

Tono hung up the phone, his heart deeply troubled. The idea that Sir Thane was involved in a plane crash chilled him to the bone. Tono couldn't handle the thought of him dying, not after the recent loss of his own father. Sir Davis had been there for him, a pillar of strength when he'd been on the brink, watching his father die.

Now he knew the reason for Brie's tears in his dream…

Tono's heart ached, and he longed to go to Brie to comfort her. But to leave Autumn now, at this fragile point in their relationship, might kill his chances with her.

And yet, if Brie needed him, he would make the trip. The warning of the dream had been too vivid to ignore.

Tono hoped he would not be forced into making that choice.

Sacrifice

Autumn called the next day and immediately apologized. "I was out of line last night. I should never have been so rude to you when you were simply being honest with me."

"So what is the reason you've rejected my advances?" he asked bluntly, needing to know the truth.

It took several moments for her to answer. "Ren...I've have never shared this with any man. I actually never thought I would have an occasion where I would ever need to."

"Go on," he encouraged when she did not elaborate.

"I can't believe I'm really going to tell you this..." She took a deep breath and blurted, "I'm a virgin. There, I said it. The embarrassing truth is finally out."

Tono hadn't considered it—not once. It shed a whole new light on her behavior toward him. "Thank you for sharing that with me, but why do I hear shame in your voice?"

"Ren, did you hear me? I'm still a virgin at my age. And it's not because I was 'saving' myself. It's a rite of passage that passed me over. Now it's like a permanent mark on my soul, letting men know I'm not desirable."

He shook his head. "Why you feel it's a mark against you is unfathomable to me. It simply means you haven't found the right man to share that part of yourself with."

"You don't understand because you've had sex—and lots of it. But when you get to be my age and you still haven't done the deed, it becomes this *huge* deal. I'm so afraid of being lousy at it that I'd almost rather not try at this point. Even worse, what if I don't like it?"

"Trust me when I say that it's worth the effort, despite your reservations. And while it may not be what you are expecting, the level of connection it creates cannot be made any other way."

"I'll admit, you have me more than a little curious, Ren, but it would be a crazy, huge step for me."

"For me as well. I have never made love to a virgin."

"Oh!" She seemed to perk up after hearing his confession.

"Does that surprise you?" he asked.

"I guess I just assumed with all the experience you've had…"

"Not too many virgins jump directly into the lifestyle, Autumn," he said with a chuckle.

She laughed at herself. "I suppose not. How does that make you feel, Ren—knowing I'm a virgin?"

He was frank with her. "I feel both intimidated and touched."

"Explain, please."

"Being your first is a profound responsibility. However, the fact no one else has touched you in that way would make our union that much sweeter."

She sighed nervously over the phone. "I'm afraid of so many things."

"Such as?"

"I could never tell you," she said, giggling nervously.

"Why not?"

"It's too embarrassing."

He chuckled warmly. "Nothing you could say would cause me to think any less of you. It might, however, give me insight into your mind-set, which will help me navigate our first time better. So what would you confide in me if I were, say...Lea?"

She scoffed at the idea, but he said nothing while he waited for her to reply.

Finally, Autumn couldn't take the silence any longer and confided, "I'm terrified of fucking up my first time. I have no idea what I'm doing."

"Fucking it up is actually the purpose of the union, so I wouldn't worry."

"Seriously, Ren. What if I suck in bed? You've had so many other women to compare me with."

"Autumn, it's impossible to suck at losing your virginity. As long as we go into this wanting to explore each other, our time together will be a success. It's not a competition. Our first time will be like no other because it's you and me."

She hesitated, needing to build up her courage to tell him what he suspected was her deepest fear. "I don't want to see the look of disgust when you see me naked."

"I find everything about you attractive."

"You say that now, but you haven't seen me totally

naked. Hell, no one has except my mother and the doctors."

"Another privilege I look forward to experiencing."

"But…"

"But what?"

She giggled to cover her unease. "There is one last thing…I know it's going to hurt."

"The gift of your virginity does come with that price. It cannot be avoided, but know that I will be as gentle as I can so your pain is not prolonged."

Autumn sighed. "I feel so dumb. Young people give up their virginity without making it a big deal. Heck, when I was younger, if any boy had talked to me the way you are now, I would have jumped at the chance without giving it a second thought."

Tono smiled to himself. "It seems you failed to realize you were putting up barriers to make certain they never tried."

"You insist on believing I was the one holding back. I wasn't, trust me. They just never showed any interest."

"I *know* you were, Autumn. I experienced it myself. You've built an impenetrable wall, even though you long to be loved."

"And why would I do that?" she protested.

"Your fear of rejection had greater power over you than your need to be loved."

"Holy shit, Ren…" she gasped. "That's deep."

"It used to define you—but that's no longer true."

"What makes you so certain?"

"We're having this conversation."

Autumn laughed, but it was cut short when she confessed, "There's one more thing."

"I'm not surprised," he answered smoothly.

"What if we do this and I fall madly in love with you, but you don't end up feeling the same way about me?"

"It's a risk we both take."

Autumn's voice trembled slightly when she told him, "To finally lose my virginity only to have the guy reject me? I don't think I could handle that."

"There are no guarantees with the heart, Autumn, but I assure you that I will never reject you. The connection remains, even if the relationship should end."

"Like you and Brie?"

Tono hesitated for a moment, unsure how to explain the relationship he had with Brie. "Similar...she and I have continued the relationship although we've moved past our romantic interests."

"But what does that mean, exactly?"

"I love her, but I think of her more like a sister now."

"Really?" Autumn questioned, sounding doubtful. "Because she's everything I wish I could be. Beautiful, talented, curious, brave—and skilled."

"You are equally beautiful, and you have your own talents. I see your curiosity beginning to blossom, and you happen to be one of the bravest women I know."

Her voice suddenly became shy. "You certainly have a way with words..."

"I speak truth."

She said softly into the phone, "I still need more time."

"As long as we are moving forward, I can be patient

a little longer." He added in a seductive tone, "If we were speaking in person right now, I would lean over and kiss you passionately without asking. Just so we are both clear about what it is I am waiting for."

"Ren…I think I'm already falling in love with you."

"I feel the same, Autumn."

Tono was reflecting on their last conversation, gratified that real progress had been made between them. That spark inside Autumn was ready to burst into flame. He was curious if she would call him that night. It was possible he might be making love to her before the evening was over.

Tono desired that connection with her in a way he'd never felt before. To finally see her femininity open and exposed to him, then to sink into the depths of her beauty and spirit… He groaned, shifting uncomfortably. Just the thought of that moment when he looked into her eyes as he breached her virginal opening had his cock aching with need for her.

He heard his phone ring, and was convinced she was picking up on his thoughts.

Instead, he saw it was Master Anderson, and the air around him suddenly grew cold.

"Hey, Nosaka."

"What is the reason for the call?" Tono asked calmly, even though he felt a sense of foreboding.

He heard the man groan. "Look, I got in a car accident today and am going to be laid up for a bit. I've been caring for Brie since the crash, but now I'm not able to and the girl can't be left alone. She's in serious trouble."

"I'm sorry to hear you were in an accident, but I'm equally concerned to learn Brie is not doing well." Tono felt ill knowing he'd failed to heed the warnings he'd been sensing, choosing instead to pursue Autumn.

"Here's the thing. Lilly's back and the witch is trouble. You may not know this, but Thane put a restraining order on his own sister. This woman is unbalanced and cannot be trusted."

Tono felt a cold chill travel down his spine. "I had no idea."

"There's no one else she needs more right now than you."

"Why do you say that?"

"I've noticed that she's constantly reminding herself to breathe, and has taken to wearing the white orchid in her hair each day. She strokes it obsessively when she thinks no one is watching."

Tono felt the air leave his lungs.

"She is not well, Nosaka."

Her soul had been crying out to him, craving his gentle guidance through her dark time, but Tono knew the cost to Autumn and him could be great.

Master Anderson continued, "Lilly poses a serious threat to Brie. Is there any way you can take a flight out today? I'm not kidding when I say time is of the essence."

Tono did not hesitate. "I will be there as soon as possible."

Master Anderson's audible sigh of relief was alarming. If he was that concerned about Brie, things were even worse than he was letting on.

The man confirmed Tono's growing fears when he said, "If anything happened to Brie, I'm afraid I'd completely lose it. She's in a fragile state right now and could shatter at any moment."

Tono closed his eyes. Brie was at her breaking point—the reason for the dream now perfectly clear. "I will make the necessary arrangements," he replied.

He thought of Autumn and his heart sank. This would be a difficult test for any couple, but especially for Autumn. Just as she was opening up to him, he was about to pull away from her—demanding she trust him on a much deeper level.

He sincerely hoped they would survive this untimely test.

Ignoring his personal concerns, Tono asked, "Should I head straight to the hospital when I arrive?"

"No, go directly to the apartment. I'll call ahead so the front desk will be expecting you. Everyone's on high alert because of Lilly's actions."

"What's going on?"

"I'll let Brie give you the details when she sees you."

"How long should I plan on staying?"

"Once I'm back on my feet, I can take over. Maybe a couple of weeks." Someone else in the room protested and Master Anderson amended his answer. "I stand corrected. The nurse is telling me it might be a bit longer."

Tono realized that he now had two difficult tasks

ahead of him. Not only would he have to break the news to Autumn, but he also needed to secure a caretaker for the home for an unspecified amount of time. It could prove exceedingly difficult. He sent out a silent plea into the Universe, trusting a solution was already forming.

"Sorry about the inconvenience," Master Anderson said.

"Not an issue. That's what family is for."

"You're a good egg, Ren Nosaka."

Tono did not feel he deserved any praise. Although he'd called Sir Davis's aunt several times and been told each time that his assistance was unnecessary, he had not trusted his instincts. He admitted to Master Anderson, "I've felt unsettled for some time, but was assured by Mrs. Reynolds that there was no need for concern."

"Understand, Nosaka, that message came as a direct order from Brie. She didn't want anyone worrying about her."

Yes. Tono had seen that in the dream... "It will actually be a relief to see her in person," he admitted. "Know that I'm glad to help in any way while Sir Davis recovers."

"I'm warning you, Nosaka, it's not looking good."

Tono felt a stab to his chest, but knew with certainty that he could help Brie.

But Master Anderson warned him that it had been a struggle keeping his emotional distance while comforting Brie. "She's a hurting unit right now; the pain is just under the surface and is easy to read even though she puts on a strong front. I don't mean to offend you when I say this, but it's imperative to comfort her without being overly comforting. Do you get what I'm saying?"

Tono knew well the sexual undercurrent that had to be kept in check. "Fortunately, I have been down this road with her before."

Master Anderson confessed to him, "It's just that I found the situation more challenging than I thought it would be. You can't help but want to wrap that little girl in your arms and take all the pain away. Yeah, so I resorted to humor and cooking soup to circumvent the issue whenever it arose. I don't know what your tools are, but they worked for me."

Tono appreciated his candidness, respecting the man for it. Truly, Brie had been in good hands under Master Anderson's care. But now it was now time for him to watch over her. "I assure you I will be thoughtful in my interactions... I desire to increase her harmony and peace, not distract from it."

"That's what she needs—along with your protection. Lilly is unbalanced."

Master Anderson had mentioned Lilly enough times for him to understand she posed a real danger to Brie, and it spurred in Tono an overpowering urge to protect her.

Luckily, with no other obligations in LA, he would be with her twenty-four/seven. Lilly would be given no access to her. "I will keep Brie safe in both mind and body, Master Anderson," he solemnly vowed.

Telling Autumn was his number one priority. With no time to waste, Tono went directly to her office rather than arranging to meet with her for lunch.

This had to be addressed in person.

When he arrived at her office, Tono went to the front desk to talk to the receptionist. "I'm Ren Nosaka, and I am here to see Autumn Day."

The woman laughed. "Doesn't she have the cutest dang name? Anytime someone asks for her I can't help but smile."

"I do find it charming," he agreed.

The woman handed him a badge. "Miss Day let me know you were coming, so you can just go on in."

Tono walked through the metal doors and looked around the large office space littered with cubicles. Thankfully, he spied Autumn waving at him in the corner.

Her face lit up as he approached her desk. "What fun to have you meet me at work, Ren! What's the special occasion? You were so mysterious on the phone."

"I actually have something I need to talk to you about," Tono said, glancing around the office. In a lower tone, he added, "Alone."

Autumn raised her eyebrows, a playful grin on her face. "Oh really?"

She naturally assumed he was flirting with her. It saddened his heart that he was here for a very different purpose. "Something's come up, Autumn."

Her smile instantly disappeared. "Something bad?"

He noticed other people listening in on their conversation. "Can we speak somewhere private?"

Autumn's hands begin to shake as she grabbed her ID badge and walked him through the maze of dividers to an outdoor break area. Thankfully, no one else was around.

"What's going on?" she asked once the door closed.

"I received a call from Master Anderson today. He was involved in a car accident and needs me to go to LA as soon as possible."

"Is he okay?"

"He's recovering but will be out of commission for a while."

"Why does he need you to go then?"

"I had no idea, but he's been taking care of Brie. The accident forced him to find a replacement."

"Why was he taking care of her?"

"As you know Thane still hasn't come out of his coma yet, which is stressful enough, but now it seems a relative of his is trying to stir trouble for Brie."

"Oh, you mean Lilly?"

"How did you know?"

"Brie mentioned something to Lea and me about her. All I know is there's bad blood between them."

"Apparently it is much worse than that, enough that Thane took out a restraining order against her. However, Lilly has broken that order."

"But why does it have to be you, Ren?" Autumn pleaded.

"Master Anderson feels I am the best person for Brie right now, and although you may not want to hear this, I agree with him."

"But just when you and I are starting to become

more serious?"

"Trust me when I say I could not be more upset about the timing of this."

She shook her head, growling under her breath. "It's going exactly like I feared. I start to let my guard down and you're running off to her."

Tono put his hands on her shoulders, gripping firmly. "It's not that way at all. I am soul-bound to Thane and Brie. They are part of my family, no different to me than your blood relatives are to you."

"Except that you fell in love with the girl."

"That is a part of our past," he stated firmly. "It does not define our relationship now."

"Then this is it for us," she cried, placing her hands on his chest. "You're going to go there and whether you want to or not, you're going to fall in love with her again."

"You're wrong," he insisted. "I'm going to protect Brie, but I assure you I will not be staying. I have no desire to. She has found her path and I..." He took his hand from her shoulder and cradled her cheek. "I have found mine."

Autumn looked into his eyes with a look of desperation and longing. "It seems like a cruel joke having you leave me now."

"It does."

"Tell me, Ren, if I forced you to choose between Brie and me, who would you choose?"

He was not willing to play such games with her and answered, "To ask me that would be like me asking you to choose between your mother who is seriously ill or me. I would *never* ask you to make that kind of choice."

She looked crestfallen. "Maybe that wasn't a fair question, but I don't think I can handle you leaving now."

He held her face in both his hands. "I'm asking you to wait for me, Autumn."

She stared up at him but shook her head when he let go. "You're asking too much. If it were your mother, it would be one thing, but this is Brie. The woman you loved and wanted to collar."

"This is also your good friend, Autumn. She is facing an unstable woman who is a danger to her while her husband lies unconscious in the hospital. Have you no compassion for the pain and fear she must be feeling?"

"Of course I do, Ren. I don't want Brie to suffer…but I don't want you to be the person to help her."

He smiled sadly. "I did not come here to discuss whether or not I was going, but I promise you I'm coming back."

"When?"

"When I feel I can safely leave her alone."

Autumn shook her head. "That's not a real answer."

"It's the best I can give you. I hope to be more specific once I'm there and can assess the situation for myself."

"You're going to fall in love with her again—I know it."

He confessed his deepest feelings to her. "I care for you in a way that I do not care for Brie."

She frowned. "Honestly, that feels like an insult to me."

"On the contrary, it's the highest compliment," he replied, unable to hide the disappointment on his face.

Autumn reached out to him when he turned to leave. "I'm sorry, Ren. I just want you to stay."

"But I have to leave."

She looked down at the ground, shaking her head sadly. "I think I'm cursed."

"No, you're not cursed. You and I have a chance at a future together. Don't let unwarranted fears change that, Autumn. I *am* coming back. Don't give up on us."

"What if the worst happens and Mr. Davis...dies... I will lose you forever."

He shook his head.

"Yes," she insisted. "You'll finally have your chance with Brie—you love her, and with a baby on the way? You would never abandon them to struggle on their own."

Tono frowned. "Mr. Davis will not die. I'm simply acting as support until he recovers."

"But what if he doesn't, Ren?"

"I don't live my life with 'what-ifs.' It wastes energy unnecessarily."

Autumn's lip trembled as she tried to be brave.

He caressed her scarred cheek tenderly. "Nothing has changed between us."

"But it *will*."

Tono put his arms around her. "If you and I are going to be a couple, then you must accept the unconventional love I have for Brie. It does not change my feelings or loyalty toward you, and jealousy will only corrupt what we have."

Tears began to roll down her cheeks. "Ren...maybe I'm wrong, but I still don't want you to leave."

He gazed into her eyes when he explained, "It comes down to whether you trust me or not. It's that simple."

"What if it were the other way around? What if I were leaving to take care of an old boyfriend?"

"I would trust you. I know your nature."

"But the heart can be fickle."

"Then you do not know your own heart, Autumn. I know mine."

Tono left Autumn feeling unsettled. He was confident in his feelings for her, but he could not control how Autumn handled this separation. It was a case where both would have to trust each other to survive this.

He spent the afternoon contacting people he knew in the area, even going so far as to reach out to the nursing staff at the Denver hospital where he had recovered after donating his kidney. But he had no luck.

Trying to find someone he trusted to look after the house and garden at the last second was proving an impossible task. Fortunately, Lea interrupted his efforts by calling.

"Is it true, Tono? Is Brie in serious trouble?"

"It's serious enough that Master Anderson requested I fly to LA immediately."

"My poor girlfriends... Autumn is broken-hearted that you're leaving and I am broken-hearted that Brie is suffering alone."

"Autumn has no reason to cry. My intentions toward her have not changed. As for Brie, she will not be alone for long."

"Is there anything I can do?"

"As a matter of fact you might be able to help me. Do you know of anyone who can take care of Master Anderson's place while I'm gone?"

"Heck yeah! Here's their number..." Lea rattled it off.

It seemed familiar to Tono, so he asked, "I take it this is someone I know?"

"You know and love her."

He chuckled lightly. "Is it your number?"

"Yep."

"What about your own place? How can you possibly take care of both?"

She laughed uncomfortably. "Actually, Tono, I wouldn't mind a temporary change of address right now. It feels like these walls are closing in around me."

"Is everything okay, Ms. Taylor?"

"Not important. Brie needs you, and by taking care of your place, it'll be my way of helping take care of Brie."

"Is it the reason you aren't there for her right now?"

Lea was slow to answer. "Brie doesn't need my drama on top of hers. I've created a deep hole I have to dig myself out of, and I can only do that here."

"I wish you well then, and thank you for your help with the house. I'll leave the key under the ceramic cat beside the door. Oh, and Ms. Taylor, try to keep Autumn's spirits up as best you can."

"I've already got a line of jokes ready for the next time we talk. I think she and I will be exchanging a lot of jokes in the coming weeks."

"At least you have each other."

"Tono…"

"Yes?"

"Please give Brie a ton of hugs for me. It's killing me to not be there for her."

"I will communicate your abundance of love, Ms. Taylor," he assured her.

After hanging up with Lea, he started packing for the extended trip. As he did so, his mind kept drifting back to Autumn and their conversation the night before. To be that close to finally connecting with her, and then to have it ripped away the very next day was exceedingly cruel.

Tono knew he was strong enough to endure the separation. The question was, could Autumn?

Toriko

O n the lonely plane ride to LA later that afternoon, as Tono kept replaying his last good-bye to Autumn, his memories naturally drifted back to that painful moment he'd told his father he was leaving Japan.

It was a powerful memory that still haunted him...

"Otosama, may I speak with you?"

"Of course, *musukosan,"* his father told him, patting the mat beside him.

Tono bowed low before crossing his legs and sitting down.

"What is this about?"

"I have come to a decision."

"Concerning?"

"My life..." Even now Tono was hesitant to voice it out loud.

"That is an immense topic."

"It is." He took a deep breath, stalling for time. Once the words were out, he could not take them back.

"Go on, *musukosan.*"

Letting his breath out slowly, Tono finally answered, "I plan to leave."

"Where are you headed?" his father asked calmly. "Osaka or Yokohama?"

"I am moving to America."

His father said nothing, the silence weighing heavily as the minutes dragged by.

Tono knew better than to fill the air with idle chatter, so he waited patiently as his father took in the news and digested it.

His father looked down at the floor, his brow furrowed. Eventually he stated, "You did not come here to ask my permission."

"No."

His father lifted his head and stared into his eyes, the gaze penetrating and hard. Tono suddenly felt the air leave his lungs when his father said in no uncertain terms, "Do not do this, *musukosan.*"

He met his father's gaze head-on. "I must."

The old man shook his head. "How can a star pupil leave his teacher when he still has much to learn? You are not ready."

"I will continue my studies in America, *Otosama.*" Tono then added, smiling to himself, "The culture there fascinates me."

"The American culture isn't the reason you are leaving Japan."

Tono nodded, unable to deny the truth.

"Your mother is *not* reason enough to leave," his father insisted.

Tono closed his eyes, stating the painful truth. "I am an unwanted distraction to my mother, and it is only getting worse the older I become."

"Her words are like gnats, irritating but not deadly," his father huffed.

"That may be true for you, but her words and actions are detrimental to me."

"Ignore them," his father stated, placing his hand on Tono's shoulder.

He looked earnestly into his father's eyes, needing him to understand the seriousness of the situation. "I cannot—and she would not allow it."

His father snorted his agreement. "No, she would not."

They sat in silence, the horrible reality of his leaving sinking in for both of them.

"You and she are similar," his father stated.

Tono hid his shock and resentment of being compared to her, and asked in a respectful tone, "How, *Otosama*?"

"You both exist in the moment while coming from opposite ends of the spectrum. She tries to correct what she views as the imbalance around her, while you simply appreciate what is. Living for the now is a rare characteristic you share."

Tono had to bite back his protest. Based on his father's assessment, he realized his mother must consider her own son to be an "imbalance." It only solidified his decision to move far away, even at the cost of losing his father.

Knowing subtleties had no place in conversations with his father, Tono did not hold back. "*Otosama*, I must leave before she emasculates me."

His father stared straight ahead, an ugly scowl on his face.

They said nothing as the sun's rays streaming in from an open window slowly advanced across the wooden floor.

Tono finally broke the silence. "*Otosama?*"

"Don't do this."

Tono felt a stab in his chest. At seventeen, he was being forced to defy his father and dishonor his entire family. Two things that seriously grieved his soul to do.

"*Otosama*. This decision was not made lightly. Please say you understand."

"Do not forsake your family and country."

Tono felt his heart crushing under the weight of his father's disapproval. "I would never forsake you."

"That is exactly what you are doing, *musukosan*," he responded harshly.

For a moment he almost lost his resolve, but Tono knew with certainty that to stay would sacrifice his very being, so he bowed low until his forehead touched the floor. "I leave you, *Otosama*, with a grieving heart. I will return each year to visit. I hope you will do the same and visit me in America. I do not want to lose yo—" His voice broke and he closed his eyes to keep his emotions at bay.

"Do not leave, *musukosan*," his father implored quietly.

Tono's throat tightened, making it difficult to say the words that would break his father's heart. "But I must."

"Then go," his father barked dismissively, turning away from him.

Tono immediately stood and started walking toward the door. He was sacrificing everything that was important to him—*Otosama*, his extended family, and his homeland—but by giving up all that he would be gaining himself.

His mother would no longer control him.

In a new land, no one would know who his father was, giving him the opportunity to find his place in the BDSM world on his own terms.

In America, he could become the man he was destined to be.

Tono held on to that truth to survive the isolation and guilt that followed him to his new country. He'd made those annual trips back to Japan as promised, and at first he was met with cold indifference, but over time his father acknowledged the growth he saw in his son and respected him for it. Although belated, his father eventually gave Tono his blessing and began his yearly pilgrimage to join his son in the US.

Tono stared out the window as the pilot came on the speaker and announced their descent in LA. He'd lost precious time with *Otosama* because of that decision to leave Japan at such a young age. Although he did not regret the move, he'd sacrificed memories with his father he would never know.

Tono thanked the staff member at the high-rise for personally letting him into the Davises' apartment. It was surreal entering their home alone, knowing that Sir Davis was in the hospital fighting for his life.

He was surprised when he heard a cat's meow from deep within the apartment. He set his suitcase on the floor and looked down the hallway. Master Anderson's small orange tabby came sauntering over to him from Brie's bedroom.

Tono knelt on one knee and held out his hand to her. Shy at first, she quickly warmed up after smelling him, familiar with his scent after having met him in Denver. She rubbed herself all over his pants, purring as she covered him in red hair.

"Lonely, are you?" he asked, chuckling lightly as he petted her.

A deep meow came from within the bedroom.

"Who's that?" Tono asked, standing up. As far as he knew, Sir Davis was not an animal person.

He stayed where he was, but called out, "I'm Ren Nosaka, a friend of the family's."

A few seconds later, Tono saw the glint of light reflecting from the luminous eyes of a huge black cat.

"And you are?"

The cat stared at him for a long time before slowly approaching. Tono felt the urge to stay still and did not kneel as the animal walked up to him. The cat circled him like a predator assessing its prey and then sat down a few feet away.

Tono sat down cross-legged facing the cat, and the two stared at each other.

"You must be Brie's protector," Tono stated.

The cat narrowed its eyes.

"I am here to assist you with that."

The cat looked the other way, its tail twitching back and forth slowly. Finally, it stood up and walked over to him, crawling into his lap. Tono petted the large furry creature, amazed at its heft and size.

He laughed unexpectedly when Cayenne jumped onto his shoulder, perching on it.

"I guess I have been officially welcomed into the family. Thank you, both."

Tono sat on the floor for a long time, soaking in the energy of the felines. He finally cleared his throat, and the cat got up from his lap. Tono got to his feet and explained, "I need to make soup before Brie arrives. I promised Master Anderson I would do that first thing."

Tono scavenged through the refrigerator and pantry, finding what he needed to make a simple ramen. He knew the broth would soothe Brie's nerves and the chicken would give her the protein she needed.

Once it was simmering away pleasantly, Tono returned to the floor and lay on his side, stroking the black cat as Cayenne watched from the arm of the couch. He heard the key in the lock, and all three turned toward it.

The door swung open, revealing a tired and dejected-looking Brie. She did not look up as she entered, dropping her purse at the entrance, the white orchid hanging loosely in her hair. She shut the door and caressed the flower, sighing loudly.

Her hand fell away as she sniffed the air several times. Turning around slowly, she gasped. "Tono?"

He looked up at her, smiling as he continued to stroke the black cat. "Didn't Master Anderson tell you I was coming?"

She shook her head.

"Well, here I am."

Brie looked stunned as she stared at the black cat. "Shadow doesn't let anyone touch him."

"Really?"

"It's the reason Master Gannon gave him to me when he passed."

Tono stopped stroking the cat. "I'm sorry you both have been through so much." Shadow looked up, meowing only once.

Slowly rising to his feet, Tono held out his arms to Brie. She walked to him with an expression of disbelief. Brie rested her head against his chest as he wrapped his arms around her. Closing his eyes, he said a silent prayer of thanks. She was alive and safe in his arms—the dream having succeeded in its purpose.

"I've missed you, Tono, but I didn't realize how much until now."

"I came as soon as Master Anderson called."

She pulled away and looked at him. "You mean to-day? You just jumped on a plane and flew over?"

"Anything for family."

"What about Autumn?"

"She understands why I'm here." He didn't explain further. There was no reason to burden Brie with their concerns.

She melted back into his arms. "You shouldn't have to put your life on hold because of me. I feel like I'm…like your mother. A burden."

Tono laughed. "Taking care of you is nothing like caring for my mother."

She looked up at him. "I don't want you to do this for me, Tono. Go back to Autumn. I know Master Anderson wants to protect me, but this is asking too much."

He looked down at her, a vision of her lifeless body in his arms coming to mind. "It is not a sacrifice to help family, toriko."

She blushed. "Well, I hope Autumn can forgive me."

"There is nothing to forgive. You have suffered a tragedy and, as family, I am here to help until Sir Davis recovers."

She smiled at the mention of her husband's name. "Sir's eyes are open, Tono. Did Master Anderson tell you?" She gazed off into space and said with conviction, "I know he hears me. I even think he visited me in a dream once."

"I'm certain he did. Your love is strong."

"Condors…" she whispered. Brie turned toward the kitchen. "What is that yumminess I smell?"

"Ramen. Master Anderson insisted I cook you soup."

Brie giggled. "He does have a thing for soup. Seemed to be making it every other day."

Tono nodded, understanding what that really meant. Master Anderson must have struggled greatly to keep himself in check, but he'd done a fine job. Brie looked healthy and her soul was intact.

"Brie, why didn't you ask me for help?"

She frowned and looked down at the floor. "I didn't think I needed it. I was so sure Sir would wake up. It wasn't until Master Anderson called me out that I even realized I wasn't okay."

"I would have been here sooner if you had asked."

She put her hand in his. "I didn't want you to come. I wanted you to make your life in Denver. You'd already given up so much for your mother and Faelan. I wanted you to finally have a chance to live."

"We are connected, Brie. Your sorrow is my sorrow."

She looked at him strangely. In a tentative voice she asked, "I remember when you called the day before the crash. You mentioned a dream."

He only nodded in answer.

"Tono, you didn't have a premonition about it…did you?"

He shook his head. "I would have said something if I had. I only had a vision of you crying tears I could not stop."

She laid her head on his shoulder. "I had no idea the night we talked that my world would fall apart the very next day."

"At least Sir Davis is showing improvement. In time

you will have your life back and be stronger for the journey."

She sighed, pressing her cheek against him.

"Have you been working on your second film to help you through this period?"

"Master Anderson had me film a scene for him, but the truth is, I haven't had the heart to do anything with my documentary."

Tono tilted her head up to look her in the eye. "You have been through a period of shock. Now you will move on to a season of living."

She smiled hesitantly.

He wrapped his arms around her again. "What else can you do to occupy your time at the hospital?"

Brie thought before answering, her voice colored with emotion. "In Italy I promised myself I would learn Italian to surprise Sir."

"That sounds like an excellent idea."

"But if he can hear me, it won't be a surprise, will it? It may even be torture for him."

He chuckled. "While it may be humorous for Sir Davis to hear you practice, I am sure it will also remind him of his family, and show him how much you love him."

Brie hugged him tighter. "How is it that you can bring light into my life so easily?"

Tono kissed the top of her head.

Brie paused for a moment before asking, "Did Master Anderson tell you about Lilly, Sir's sister?"

"Only that Sir Davis felt the need to put a restraining order on her after China, and yet she is breaking that order now. Master Anderson warned me that she is unstable, and that is the reason I will remain by your side until she is apprehended by the police."

Brie shivered, confessing, "I'm scared of her, Tono. Really scared…"

He squeezed her tighter and felt Brie begin to relax in his embrace. "I don't know what's happened, but I promise I will not let that woman hurt you."

"Lilly is just like her mother was—maybe worse."

"A lethal person for the soul."

"Yes, that's the perfect way to put it."

He nodded. "I believe some people allow in a darkness so black that they become rabid inside, destroying others in their desperation to escape what they've created. I do not know her personally, but I feel she is one of those. You can't penetrate that kind of darkness, Brie. You can only run from it."

"It's so strange that Sir is related to Ruth and Lilly. How is it he is normal and they are not?"

"He controlled what he let into his life. It was a conscious choice he made."

"So you don't think there's hope for Lilly?"

"Where you are concerned? No. Based on her actions after the crash, she's on a mission to destroy you. Nothing you do will cause her to deviate from that task."

Brie shivered again, asking, "Even if I give her what she wants?"

"What would stop her from coming back later and demanding more?"

He noticed Brie was careful in how she answered him. "Lilly promised she wouldn't for someone else's sake."

"Do you trust her as a person?"

"No!"

"Then why would trust any promise she makes?"

"But you have no idea what she has threatened to do."

"Brie, a predator goes for the jugular once its prey shows signs of weakness. She will not stop."

"Tono, she can ruin us."

"But you will survive the storm she creates."

Brie seemed frustrated by his answer.

"You *will* survive this," he insisted.

She shook her head. "What she holds over us will not only hurt me, but it will permanently ruin Sir's reputation. There will be no coming back from it."

"I can't imagine how this woman could have that kind of power over you both."

Brie's bottom lip trembled. "If she's lying, it is a plot so evil I can't fathom it, and if it is true...I don't know what I'll do."

He felt her panic start to rise. Holding her closer, he whispered soothingly, "Hush those thoughts, toriko."

Tono had come thinking he was prepared for anything. It had only taken a few short minutes to be humbled by the situation Brie was facing. She was legitimately frightened, and it seemed she had good reason to be.

Lilly meant harm and was already creating rifts of fear and doubt inside Brie.

"We will weather what comes. You are not alone."

When Brie gazed up with those big, trusting, doe-like eyes, his breath caught for a moment.

New Season

The next morning, when Brie led Tono through the doors of the hospital, he felt a moment of unease.

She picked up on it and asked him, "Is it hard visiting a hospital when you were so recently a patient in one?"

He smiled slightly. "Although the staff was exceptional, I don't care for the sterile environment."

Brie nodded. "I've done everything I can to enhance Sir's environment because I feel exactly the same way."

Tono was welcomed by one of the nurses as they approached the ICU. "Feel free to join Mrs. Davis, Mr. Nosaka. Brad Anderson already informed us that Mr. Davis's other adopted brother was arriving today."

Tono looked at her questioningly.

Brie took Tono's hand and squeezed it. "It's true that Sir has a large family. Thank you for adding him to the list."

He nodded to the nurse. "Thank you, Ms...?"

"Abby," the nurse said with a grin.

"A pleasure," he stated, giving her a slight bow.

Brie led him directly to Sir Davis's hospital room, bursting with excitement. "Every day is a chance that Sir will awake. I feel that even more now that you're here."

Tono walked into the room and saw Sir Davis lying there, and for a moment he had a vision of his father in the same condition, struggling for his last breath.

Brie hugged him. "I know, Tono. I was reminded of your father too when I first saw him."

Tono looked down at her, tears welling in his eyes. "I don't think I will ever reconcile *Otosama's* death. Time does not ease the pain."

Her bottom lip trembled. "I understand." She looked at Sir. "If I lose him, I'd be lost."

Tono put an arm around her. "Unlike my father, Sir Davis will recover."

He then walked over to the bed and spoke to Sir, believing the man could hear everything being said. "Sir Davis, it's Ren Nosaka. I've come to watch over Brie while you recover." Tono reached out and took his hand, holding it firmly. "You are my family."

Brie smiled at him, her eyes sparkling. "Thank you, Tono."

"I will let you have some time alone with Sir Davis while I speak to the nursing staff. They are a wealth of knowledge that rarely gets tapped."

Brie nodded, pulling up a chair next to the bed.

"I also have an errand, Brie. Will you feel safe if I leave you here for a few hours?"

"Of course. I won't budge from this spot until you return."

After speaking with the staff, Tono felt assured Brie

was safe and left on his errand. His mission was to find a laptop for Brie. She needed something with the same power and capabilities as her computer at home to aid her in completing the documentary.

His father had left him a small portion of money after his death, and Tono had been uncertain how to spend it up to this point.

It only made sense to spend it on Brie's documentary—her dream. In a sense, his father's gift would counter the disservice he'd shown Brie at the Collaring Ceremony when *Otosama* had dismissed her as unworthy.

Tono found joy and satisfaction in supporting Brie with her career. This was the perfect opportunity to not only help her move forward during this difficult time, but to support her professional endeavors. He was certain his father would approve.

He could tell that sitting in that hospital room day after day was slowly killing Brie inside, even though she could not see it. To reconnect with her dreams and ambition would reignite the fire in her soul.

Brie was a talented filmmaker, but she had let that fall away in the chaos.

Tono thought back on his own experience, when Sir Davis had insisted he find a way to continue his Kinbaku. The man had been right, and that sage advice had saved Tono's sanity when things had gone south with his mother.

It was fitting that he would play the same role for Brie now.

After spending an hour talking with a salesman about the capabilities of the various laptops, he finally settled on one he felt could do the job now and would grow with her in the future.

Tono took the time to go to another store to have it gift wrapped. To his way of thinking, the presentation was as important as the gift itself.

Before heading back to the hospital, he stopped at a local park lined with palm trees and called Autumn.

"Hello."

"It's good to hear your voice, Autumn."

She paused for a second, giving him momentary reason to worry before she said, "I feel the same, Ren. How is Brie doing?"

"In worse shape than I thought. However, I'm setting things in place so that she can concentrate on her work while watching over Sir Davis. She's become like a prisoner at the hospital, but I'm attempting to change that."

"I'm glad to hear it. Truly."

"How are you doing?"

He heard her voice catch when she said, "I'm...struggling. I wish I could tell you everything's fine, but I miss you and I'm unsure how I'm going to handle your long absence."

"One day at a time, Autumn. You and I will get through this one day at a time."

"It really does help to hear your voice," she confessed.

Tono smiled to himself. "This call was selfish on my part. I just needed to hear your voice."

"I'm glad you called. I want you to take good care of yourself—and Brie."

"I will. You do the same with you and Lea."

She laughed. "We're a mess, us two. But we keep each other laughing."

"Good."

The first hurdle of their separation had been cleared, and it gave Tono reason to hope.

He returned to the hospital holding the wrapped box and a second package in his hands. Nurse Abby smiled at him as he entered the ICU. He nodded to her, understanding her important role in Sir Davis's recovery, as well as Brie's well-being.

When he entered the room, he announced to Brie, "I have a gift for you."

She looked up and then put her hands to her mouth in surprise. "What's this? It's so beautiful, Tono."

Tono handed over the box covered in cherry blossoms and pink ribbon.

"Why would you do this?" she asked, staring at the package, a stunned smile on her lips.

"You'll understand when you open it. It's actually a practical item."

Brie placed it on the arms of the chair beside Sir Davis's bed and spoke to him as she stared down at it. "Oh Sir, isn't the wrapping paper so pretty? I almost hate to tear it."

Tono thought back on his dream. Rather than considering the cherry blossoms a warning, he'd chosen to think of them as a symbol of hope. The vision had prompted him to make the trip, and he was deeply grateful for it.

When he noticed she still hadn't opened the gift, he told her, "Please rip into it. You can't enjoy the gift until you do."

Brie nodded and started carefully pulling at the tape to preserve the paper.

"No, Brie. Rip into it," he insisted.

She smiled at Tono with a twinkle in her eye as she tore the paper apart. She stared at the printed box in disbelief. "You didn't…" Brie looked up at him, shaking her head. "You shouldn't have, Tono." She turned to Sir Davis and explained, "Tono has gifted me a top-of-the-line laptop, Sir, so I will be able to upload all my programs and work on the documentary here—with you."

Brie looked back at Tono, still shaking her head.

"You both know how much I respect your talent. It pleases me to be a part of the process in whatever way I can."

She held up the box. "But this? It's way too much. It must have cost you a fortune, Tono."

"It was part of my father's inheritance. I'm positive he would approve."

He saw the understanding in her eyes. She looked down at it, lightly caressing the box with reverence.

"I want you to finish that second documentary so the world can breathe in its positive message."

"I will, Tono," she declared, her gaze focused on the box. "I will honor you and your father with my efforts."

"Excellent," he answered. "I bought something else to go with it. It's out by the nurses' station."

Her head perked up. "More?"

He glanced toward Sir Davis with a mysterious grin. "It's a surprise."

Brie looked past him to see Abby holding up another package.

"I'll be right back, Sir," she said, rushing out of the room.

Tono took the opportunity to speak to Sir Davis privately. "I will do everything in my power to protect her from Lilly." Tono put his hand on Sir Davis's shoulder. "You can trust that I will not fail you or Brie, I give you my solemn promise."

The monitor showed a momentary spike before settling back down to a steady beat. Tono felt a very real connection with Sir Davis. He was certain the man was cognizant of his presence.

Brie burst back into the room grinning as she held up DVDs for learning Italian and a set of headphones to go with them. It thrilled him—her joy was his joy.

Tono told Brie, "You have every reason to believe Sir Davis will make a full recovery. I can feel his spirit fighting to return."

She threw her arms around him, still holding the gifts. "It means so much to hear you say that. Everyone tries to be careful not to get my hopes up." She smiled down at her husband. "But I know he hears everything I say. I've been careful not to dishonor him in my words or my thoughts."

"As a good submissive should."

Brie smiled and gave him a reverent bow. "You've changed my life by coming here. Thank you."

"No thanks are necessary. Seeing you smile is enough."

She would never know that images of her lifeless face still haunted him. Seeing her alive and well truly was a priceless gift to Tono.

Brie looked at her laptop and asked, "What are you planning to do while I'm working on my documentary?"

"I plan to set up photo shoots with some of my top models over the years. Master Anderson's home will be the perfect backdrop as I ease back into Kinbaku."

"Do you have plans to travel again?"

"Eventually, yes. However, I have to give my body time to heal before I can take on the rigors of a tour. I also want to give Autumn and I more time to get to know each other."

"So it is going well between you two?" she asked with an impish smile.

"We have strong feelings for each other."

"I knew she was something special when I met her. Then when you pulled that veil from her face the first time you met? Well, that was shocking and powerful, Tono."

"It was a shock for us both. I was completely drawn in by the strong connection I felt for her. Autumn is truly unique."

"I could tell there was an instant connection that first day." Brie laughed. "I've been waiting not so patiently ever since for you two to announce you're formally dating. I have to assume Italy lived up to your expectations?"

He smirked, amused by her interest, but answered cryptically, "It was promising."

"And when you returned home?"

"More promising."

"I'm so glad. It helps me immensely knowing you two are happy." Brie put her hands to her heart, her eyes sparkling with joy. "You mentioned your health. Have you been healing well, Tono?"

"I have to respect my limitations, but they lessen each month."

"Good." She abruptly changed the subject, asking him, "Have you had a chance to speak to Mr. Wallace lately?"

Tono kept his expression pleasant for Brie's sake. He knew things were not going well for the Wolf Pup personally, but saw no reason to share that with her now. He chose instead to concentrate on the positive by telling her, "We meet up weekly these days, and every time I've seen continued improvement in his health. I'm impressed how far he's come from that husk of a man we encountered in the hospital."

"I'm glad to hear that. I've been worried about him..." Brie seemed to be holding something back. It was quite possible she already knew some of what was going on, but Tono just smiled in response.

"Have you seen Lea?"

"I have. In fact, she is watching my home and wanted me to do this." Tono gave Brie a hug, imagining he was passing on Lea's friendship and good thoughts to Brie.

She smiled when he let go, lamenting, "Dang, I miss that girl."

"Lea misses you as well, but was kind enough to take on the responsibility of the house so I could come without delay. She wanted you to know she was here with you in spirit."

Brie looked into his eyes, searching for something more. He kept a peaceful expression under her scrutiny. "Is she okay, Tono?"

He could not lie to her, but stated simply, "She did share that she has some personal business that keeps her in Denver."

Brie dropped her gaze, mumbling, "I was afraid of that."

Not wanting her to worry he added, "But Autumn told me they've been trading a lot of jokes these days."

"I'm glad that Autumn can be there for her." Brie looked up at Tono sadly. "I really hate that at a time when we all really need each other, none of us can be there for one another."

Position of Power

To distract Brie from her mounting worries, Tono insisted on starting a new routine at the hospital.

Sitting down next to Sir's bed, they worked side by side—Brie with her heavy-duty laptop and Tono with his much smaller tablet. After he was done looking through his emails, Tono glanced over and noticed Brie's eyes were glued to her screen. She had quite the passionate look on her face.

"Good footage?"

She blushed as she took off her headphones and smiled at him. "Yeah, it was the one I recently shot with Master Anderson and Boa." She looked at the screen again and bit her bottom lip before exclaiming, "It's so dang hot…"

Brie looked at Sir. "You remember that night I left to film at the Haven, Sir? I had no idea just how sexy the single spotlight in the dark would be as a setting for these two. I didn't think I would have much to work with, but…" she fanned herself, "these two men really know how to command the stage."

She grinned at Tono before sliding her headphones back on.

Tono chuckled to himself as he opened up a new email that had just popped up on his screen. He was thrilled to see it was from Marianna, a favorite model he'd worked with during the nationwide tour the year before.

Dear Tono Nosaka,

I cannot tell you how excited I am that you are back doing the art you love and were born to create. I'm honored that you have asked me to come to your home in Denver to work with you.

I say with a full heart that I look forward to being in your presence again.

Unfortunately, I am visiting my parents overseas for the summer but will be coming out to the US in the fall, and would dearly love to reserve a time to work with you then.

I can just imagine how beautiful the fall colors will be in the mountains there. What a perfect backdrop for your Kinbaku art.

I was heartbroken to hear of your father's passing, but I know he is with you in spirit as you tie every knot.

My blessings to you, Tono Nosaka.

With much respect,
Marianna

Even though the mention of his father still wounded him, Marianna was right. His father would be anxious to see Tono applying the skills he'd painstakingly passed on and perfected in his only son.

Tono looked up to see Brie walking over to Sir to take his hand. "Will today be the day, Sir? Is this the day you turn your eyes toward me and squeeze my hand?" She leaned over and kissed him on the cheek before turning toward Tono.

He heard her stomach rumble and looked up at the clock to see that it was twelve. Noon was a significant hour. It was the moment the sun was at its zenith and had the most power—exposing everything under it with its bright light.

Tono narrowed his eyes in thought. Standing up, he asked her, "Is there someplace good we can go for lunch?"

Brie shook her head. "The only place I'd recommend is the café, but that's where Lilly cornered me."

"Perfect."

She looked troubled and frowned. "Why?"

"If Lilly is stalking you, returning to that place will send the clear message that you are not alone and you are not afraid."

Brie let out a nervous sigh. "The idea of that frightens me, Tono. Especially since her deadline is drawing near."

"All the more reason to show her that you are not afraid. It's better to meet the enemy in a position of power."

She was trembling when she took the hand he offered. "I'm willing, Tono, as long as you're with me."

"Good." He turned his attention back to her husband. "Sir Davis, as you've just heard, I will be taking Brie out for lunch. Should we happen to see Lilly, I will call the authorities so she can finally be apprehended. I give you my solemn promise not to put Brie in harm's way, but I'm sure you agree it's time to bring this to a close."

Before they left, Brie leaned over and tenderly kissed Sir Davis on the lips. "Don't worry, I promise to come back soon." She automatically stared at the monitor but didn't see a change. She looked at Tono and shrugged, but he could tell she was hurt.

As he led her out of the hospital, Tono asked her, "You do realize the reason you see no change in the monitor?"

She shook her head sadly.

"You are his heartbeat. Sir Davis lives and breathes for you."

Brie stopped for a moment, crushing her head against his shoulder in an attempt to keep her tears at bay. When she finally looked up, she told him in a voice full of emotion, "Thank you, Tono. I needed to hear that."

He put his arm around her as they walked together in silence out of the sterile environment of the hospital and into the sunshine.

Brie lifted her head and purred, "I love the sun."

"You've seen far too little of it. I hope that changes today."

A shiver coursed through Brie, but she nodded and

continued on.

"Walk with your head up and a smile on your face. If she is anywhere near, your lack of concern should unsettle her."

Brie forced a smile.

"She does not control you, toriko."

Brie digested his words, looking at him a few moments later with renewed confidence. "No, she does not," she agreed. "I *want* her to feel unsettled."

She stood a little taller as she shielded her eyes from the bright rays of the sun. "I have played the scared mouse long enough. It's time I take on the role of a huntress—like Cayenne."

"Like Cayenne," he agreed, touched by her act of courage.

When they entered the restaurant, Tono purposely picked a table next to the window, explaining to her, "If Lilly is out there, I want to make sure she sees us."

Brie leaned forward and whispered, "But, Tono, what if it provokes her?"

"The only way she will expose herself is if we force her hand. Until she's in custody, you're not safe. We have to push her to act, but on our terms."

"How has she avoided capture so easily?"

"She appears to take after your husband in intellect."

Brie nodded, telling him, "You should have seen the two in China—both so adept at manipulating the other."

"It sounds…uncomfortable."

"It was actually frightening to witness."

Tono felt Brie's fear start to rise as she thought back on her experiences in China. In response, he placed his hand on hers and smiled warmly. "We're here to enjoy a good lunch together."

Brie looked into his eyes, taking in a deep breath. "Yes, I need to keep focused."

He raised up his hand and ordered for the both of them when the waitress swung by. The young woman winked at Tono as she grabbed the menus. "If you need anything else, you just give me a holler, hon."

Brie giggled after the waitress left. "Looks like you have another admirer, Tono."

He chuckled in response, but his thoughts instantly drifted to Autumn. He wondered how her day was going and looked forward to talking to her later that night—hopefully with the news that the Lilly threat had been eliminated.

While they ate, Tono steered the conversation, asking Brie to describe each of the scenes she'd filmed for her second documentary. It was an easy way to get her mind focused on something other than Lilly.

As she talked, he saw once again the excitement and passion he'd grown to love in her. Brie's eyes lit up when she shared interesting tidbits about each scene. It reminded him of old times when he'd sat in the pizza parlor while she gushed on and on about her ideas for the original documentary.

"...of course, I won't be able to use all of them, but I *would* if I could," Brie said with a grin. "Each scene is precious to me, like a jewel. I really dislike the fact Mr. Holloway has the power to cut them out."

"That would be difficult, especially if you feel strongly about the scene in question."

"Oh, Tono, it is. I've actually cried tears."

"Have you thought of gathering the ones that don't make the final cut and creating a short film to highlight them? A bonus of sorts for fans of your work."

Her eyes sparkled. "I love that idea! It could be on my own time and on my own dime. That way none of my scenes have to be lost." Brie looked out the window, a dreamy expression on her face. "Someday when I'm rich and famous...I'll do that," she vowed.

"Good, just remember to mention me in the credits," Tono joked.

Brie took his hand and gently squeezed it. "Of course you will be in the credits. Your enthusiasm and support have spurred me on. I can't thank you enough for all you've done."

He shook his head, chuckling. "It's been selfish on my part—longing to have a small part in the masterpieces you create."

She blushed. "You always have a way of making me feel good, even when things seem bleak."

"It's a characteristic you have as well," he replied, smiling as he stood up. "Shall we head back to the hospital and let Mr. Davis know you are safe and sound?"

"You didn't see any sign of her, did you?"

"No, but it's time we head back. I don't want Sir Davis worrying unnecessarily."

"Agreed. Although we failed to spot her, this was a great idea. I really needed to get out and bask in the sunshine."

"You certainly did," he agreed, guiding her out of the

café.

"Thanks for coming," the waitress called out.

Tono turned and gave her a small bow of thanks.

The woman glanced away, fanning herself.

"Yep, you've still got it, Tono," Brie said, laughing lightly.

Once outside, Tono was immediately hit with the feeling of being watched. In a calm voice he told Brie, "She's here, but keep walking as if we aren't aware."

He could feel the darkness near him, like a cold shadow on his soul. He glanced around nonchalantly, hoping to catch sight of her, but saw nothing. He laughed as he stopped before a small flower garden near the sidewalk and pointed it out to Brie while he dialed the emergency number and explained where they were. After getting assurances that a police car was on its way, Tono picked a flower and handed it to Brie.

She kept an outer look of calm as she accepted it, but asked in a frightened whisper, "Do you see her?"

"No, but the police are on their way." Wrapping one arm around Brie, he continued strolling back to the hospital. "We'll just take it slow to give them extra time to check the perimeters. Hopefully, this will soon be over."

Tono's plan worked, but not in the way he'd anticipated. Although the police had been unable to find any trace of Lilly, it was just as Tono suspected: She not only had been there but had observed their every move, spurring a phone call to Brie late that night.

Tono knew something was up when he saw the look of terror on Brie's face when she answered the phone.

"Lilly…" Brie said breathlessly.

They'd been waiting for contact, so Tono grabbed the mini-recorder her lawyer insisted Brie use in case the woman called her directly.

Brie took the recorder from him, switching the phone to speaker. She closed her eyes as Lilly's voice filled the room. "…I was surprised to see you acting so smug today, Mrs. Davis. Have you given up on Thane and found a new lover already?"

Brie was literally shaking. Tono knew that fear would transfer to her voice so he scribbled a quick note and showed it to her.

Keep calm and try to keep her talking.

"What do you want, Lilly?"

"You seem to need a reminder about what's at stake here."

"I understand exactly what you plan to do." She glanced at Tono nervously.

Tono wrote another note, giving her an encouraging smile as he showed it to her.

Exude confidence.

Brie nodded, taking a deep breath.

"Really?" Lilly snarled. "You're certainly not acting like it. While I plan to let the press in on what Thane has done, as an added little bonus, I thought it might be fun to give your parents a heads-up before I do."

"Don't you dare," Brie cried, her voice tinged with

anger now.

Lilly's laughter was malicious and cruel. "What? Don't you think your parents will still support Thane after they find out what's happened?"

Tono put his arm around Brie and leaned in, whispering, "Don't let her draw you in."

Taking his advice, she assumed control of the conversation. "In the end, I can't stop you, Lilly."

"Actually you can, but now it's going to cost you more. I *don't* like being trivialized."

"I'm done playing your games because I believe nothing I do will change the outcome."

"Oh, that's not true. If you make the mistake of choosing to do nothing, the outcome is set and you will have caused your own ruin when you could have easily avoided it."

"I don't believe you."

Lilly's gloating laughter gave Tono the chills.

"So here's the new deal, Mrs. Davis," she replied. "In response to your insolence. You produce what I've requested *and* gift me Thane's Lotus. That should hit the bastard where it hurts."

There was a long pregnant pause before Brie asked, "And if I don't?"

"I have something else in mind and..." Lilly answered in an ominous tone, "and it doesn't involve money."

"What then?"

Tono could feel Brie's fear returning and wrapped both arms around her in support.

Lilly laughed. "It's a surprise, buttercup. Don't be

stupid, there's far more at stake here than you know. If I don't get what I'm asking for, you'll end up being sorry in ways you never imagined."

"Vague threats come from a place of weakness."

"You really want to test that theory?" Lilly answered chillingly.

"I'm not afraid of you, Lilly."

"You should be."

Before Brie could respond, Lilly ended the call by saying, "Say hello to your new lover boy for me. I know he's listening."

After Lilly hung up, Brie tossed the phone away from her as if it were poison. "Tono, you don't think she would really contact my parents, do you?"

Before Tono could answer, the phone rang again. Brie turned white when she saw who was calling. "It's my mom," she whimpered.

"Don't answer it," Tono advised. "Let it go to voicemail. Better to let her leave a message and find out exactly what she knows so you can form an appropriate reply."

Brie nodded. After several rings, it switched to her voicemail and took several minutes before the phone dinged to let her know a message had been left.

"I'm afraid to listen…" she said nervously. "Lilly is doing exactly what she said she'd do, Tono."

"Be brave. We can't fight against this until we know."

Brie nodded with tears in her eyes as she picked up the phone and hit the message button. He was encouraged when she left the speaker on so both of them could listen to it.

"Brianna, I have no idea who sent this, but you are so lucky your father didn't see it first. What's going on with you? We haven't heard from you in weeks and now we get this email? You need to call me. I deserve to know what's happened because if this is true... Brianna, I'm afraid I'm going to have to call the police." She paused for a moment before stating in disgust, "His own sister?"

"Oh god, she really did it," Brie cried, turning to Tono with a look of panic.

"Before you speak with your mother, I recommend you talk to Mr. Thompson. He needs to hear your recorded conversation with Lilly as well as this message from your mother."

"Yes," Brie agreed dully, dropping the phone back on the couch.

"Take heart that Lilly has exposed herself with this stunt."

"At the cost of my parents..."

Tono embraced her protectively. "They will see through the lies."

"Not my dad, Tono. He'll never let it go."

"Breathe, toriko. First we speak to the lawyer, then you call you mother and see if you can douse the flames of Lilly's deceit."

When he let go of her, Brie picked up her cell and called Mr. Thompson, who immediately set up a meeting.

While Tono was driving her to the office, he asked her to explain what was really going on.

"I can't. You know too much already."

He was further put off when the lawyer requested he remain in the waiting room.

"It's for the best, Tono," Brie assured him. "The fewer people who know, the better for everyone."

He stayed behind to appease her and sat down, picking up a magazine with disinterest. Flipping through it, however, he saw something unusual and backtracked until he found the page again. On it was a handwritten message in pen with decidedly male penmanship.

I hate being kept in the dark. ~BA

Tono stared down at it, certain that Master Anderson had been in this very room, exiled from a meeting with Brie's lawyer, having no clue what was going on with Lilly. It made it easier to bear, but also gave him greater reason to worry.

What secret was Brie keeping that had the potential to tear her apart?

When the lawyer came out of the office with Brie, he walked directly over to Tono and shook his hand firmly. "That was brilliant on your part. We now have a phone number to track her movements by, which I have given to the investigator on the case." He seemed confident when he said, "With any luck, she should be safely behind bars soon."

"What about the recording?" Tono asked.

"While it's not solid evidence due to the vagueness of her threats, it does show intent which the police can use to justify increasing their presence."

Brie walked over to Tono and leaned against him, looking emotionally beaten. "Even though I still have to face my mom, I feel hopeful we can defeat Lilly for the first time." She looked up at him and smiled weakly. "That is worth the price."

He was relieved she felt that way and nodded to Mr. Thompson before escorting Brie out of the building.

"So overall it sounds like your lawyer is optimistic."

"He is. He also gave me some information that I needed to hear."

"I suppose I'm not allowed to ask?"

"I'm going to tell you anyway," Brie said stubbornly, pulling out a journal from her purse to show him. "I had Mr. Thompson locate an expert to analyze the handwriting in Sir's journal."

"Why would you do that?"

She looked down at the leather-bound journal. "There was something in here that was extremely hurtful pertaining to Sir's time in China. I needed to know if they were Sir's words or not." Brie sighed deeply. "It turns out the expert found it difficult to verify initially because the penmanship is so close in structure, but after careful analysis between the two samples, he is convinced it is not Sir's handwriting." She kissed the journal, a look of relief on her face.

"If it wasn't his, whose was it?"

Brie said with disdain, "Lilly's."

Tono couldn't hide his shock. "She faked an entire journal?"

Brie shook her head. "No, she wrote one line in it."

"You're telling me she stole his personal journal and

wrote in it?"

"That's exactly what happened, and she did it because she hoped one day I would read it."

Tono shook his head, horrified by the calculated act.

Brie looked at the journal again as she flipped through the pages. "I remember seeing a note she'd written to Sir when they'd first met, and her handwriting reminded me of his. At the time I thought it was sweet—highlighting the fact they were siblings." She stopped on one page, staring hard at the single sentence written there. "I never suspected for a second that she would use it against me in the most hateful way."

Brie shut the journal and continued walking on in silence, but Tono noticed how tightly she hugged the journal to her chest and the slight smile on her lips.

He understood it was a personal victory against Lilly and trusted it would be the first of many.

Once they arrived at the apartment, Brie asked him to listen in on her phone call with her mother, asking for his guidance during the call.

"Aren't you afraid I will hear things you don't want me to know?"

"Tono, it's not prudent to keep this from you. Besides, if I can't trust you, then who can I trust?"

He nodded, agreeing with her assessment. "My one piece of advice, Brie, is to let her do the talking. Answer only what's required and don't go into detail. No reason to complicate her life by giving away more information than necessary."

"Got it." Brie hit dial and switched it to speaker phone.

Her mother immediately picked up. "Brianna, what's going on? I have been sitting by the phone all this time waiting to hear back from you."

"Mom, before I say anything, I need to know exactly what happened."

"What happened? I'll tell you what happened! I received an email from someone calling themselves Brianna's Friend. In the email were pictures of your husband with another woman. Both of them looked disheveled and his hands are on her in all three photos."

Brie shivered but sounded calm when she asked, "Mom, those photos… what are they doing in them?"

"They show the two walking down a street in some foreign city—oriental by the looks of the lettering. They both appear to be quite drunk."

Brie said nothing, so Tono nudged her gently, encouraging her to speak.

"Mom, besides the photos, was there anything else attached in the email?"

"Yes, it came with a disgusting message."

"What did it say?"

"Mr. and Mrs. Bennett, I felt the need to inform you that your daughter is married to a monster. These photos were taken months before their wedding. This is Thane with his biological sister. She is pregnant with his child."

Brie let out a small gasp. Tono took her face in his hand and gazed deep into her eyes, helping her to regain her center.

"Brianna, tell me this isn't true!"

"No, Mom, it's a lie. A terrible, vicious lie. You can't believe a word that woman says."

"What woman?"

"Thane's half-sister. Lilly is out to destroy us."

"Are you *positive* she's lying?" her mother asked, clearly unhinged by the news.

"I know she is, Mom. She's trying to hurt me by going to you."

"But, Brianna, how do you explain these pictures?"

"Thane said his sister insisted on celebrating when she thought their mother had opened her eyes. He told me that the two of them got drunk that night. I'm willing to bet those photos you have show Sir simply trying to get them both back to the hotel in one piece."

"I'm not sure..." she replied. Tono guessed she was staring at the photos. "How do you explain their disheveled state?"

Brie looked at Tono for a moment before answering vaguely, "Foreign countries can be dangerous for drunk Americans."

"Do you have any idea what would have happened if your father had gotten a hold of this email instead of me?"

"I do. I have thought of nothing else. I'm just eternally grateful it found its way to you first."

"Brianna, why would this woman accuse Thane of such a thing?"

Tono could hear the anxiety in her mother's voice and scribbled a note.

Assure her.

"Mom," Brie said gently, "Lilly is crazy like her mother. She wanted to hurt us, but her last-ditch effort didn't work because of you. I can't thank you enough."

"You don't know how close she came, little girl. Your father is pulling into the driveway as we speak."

Tono quickly wrote another note.

Evidence.

Brie quickly instructed, "Mom, can you forward the email to me before you delete it? I may need it for evidence against her."

"Brianna, you know I hate keeping things from your father."

"I trust you to do what you feel is best."

In the background they could hear the sound of a door opening.

"Is that you, dear?" her mother called out before hanging up the phone.

Brie stared at Tono in stunned silence for several moments before uttering, "Tono, there are pictures…"

She grabbed her tablet and opened the email her mother had just sent. Attached to it were the three photographs her mother had talked about. Tono stared at them closely, noting the disoriented look on Sir Davis's face, and the way he held Lilly close to him.

Lilly, on the other hand, was smiling up at him strangely.

Brie enlarged the photos so Tono could study them more closely. Lilly didn't have the look of a drunken woman. Her stare was far too intense. It gave Tono chills to look at it.

He also noticed that the woman seemed to be holding Sir Davis's hands against her body, as if she were posing him. It only affirmed his suspicions that Lilly had staged the pictures.

While he was still trying to wrap his head around the horrifying accusation being levied against Sir Davis, one thing was evident based on the photos alone. "She planned this, Brie. These pictures were plotted out."

Brie actually smiled at his pronouncement. "I'm comforted to know she took pictures that night. In trying to prove his guilt, Lilly shared evidence that proves hers. Maybe she isn't as smart as she thinks."

Tono put his arm around Brie's shoulders and cautioned, "Although it is obvious this is a scam, Lilly still poses a real threat to you. Irrational people are capable of causing considerable damage."

"I understand, Tono," Brie said, smiling, "but I can't wait to go to the hospital in the morning and tell Sir the good news! Lilly thought she could hurt me by leaking it to my parents, but she only hurt herself. I'm sending these to Mr. Thompson right now."

While Tono was glad to see the weight lifted off Brie, he wouldn't feel the same until Lilly was in the hands of the authorities. That look in her eyes as she stared up at Sir in the photos chilled him to the bone.

Dancing in the Rain

"I live for our nightly phone calls."

"It is the highlight of my day as well, Autumn."

She let out a happy sigh. "Maybe we can do a video chat tomorrow? I think seeing you would also help with this whole separation thing."

"That's a good suggestion. I'll upload an app on my phone so we can do that next time," Tono agreed.

"Ren..."

"Yes, Autumn."

"I do trust you."

"I'm glad to hear it."

"Please give Brie my best."

"I will. Take care of yourself until we chat."

"Thanks for calling."

"My pleasure, Autumn."

Brie had walked in at the tail end of the call and quickly retreated. Afterward, Tono went to find out what she wanted.

He heard her softly sobbing in her bedroom as he

approached the closed door. "Brie?"

The sound suddenly stopped.

"Brie," he called out again, slowly opening the door when she didn't answer. "What's up?"

"Nothing," she replied, but she smashed her face into her pillow and started to sob even louder.

Tono slowly entered the room. He could instantly tell Brie had moved nothing since the plane crash; everything remained in place like a museum waiting for Sir Davis's return. It was eerie, reminding him of the story of Sleeping Beauty.

He asked her lightly, "What's with the dead flowers?"

She pulled her head out of the pillow and glanced at them. "Ms. Clark sent them to me. I didn't have the heart to get rid of them after they…" She struggled, seemingly unable to utter the word "died." The tears threatened to start up again so she distracted herself by pointing out the nightstand covered in belts.

"Sir told me to leave them there to celebrate his return."

Tono smiled kindly, although his heart was breaking for her. There was so much love and pain here. "Ah."

She glanced around the bedroom. "Everything here both comforts and torments me."

Tono nodded in understanding. "Is that why you were crying?"

She shook her head, unable to look him in the eye.

Knowing he couldn't force it out of her, he decided on a different tactic. "Would you like some tea?"

Brie smiled sadly and nodded.

While he boiled the water, Brie came out of her

room and sat cross-legged on the marble floor next to Shadow and began petting the cat. Her forlorn expression concerned Tono, considering her earlier excitement.

Once the tea was ready, he walked over to her. When she started to get up, he stopped her. "No, no. Stay where you are. I will join you on the floor."

He knelt down before handing her a cup, then settled on the other side of Shadow. Brie took a long whiff of the green tea before sipping, and purred, "I love your tea, Tono. Whenever I make it myself, it never tastes quite as good."

He chuckled, taking a sip. "I'm sure that's not true."

"It is. You have a special knack I don't." She still was refusing to look him in the eye.

They sipped the hot liquid in silence. Tono waited until the right moment to speak, using her sub name to emphasize their deep connection and history. "What are you thinking about, toriko?"

Brie smiled at him hesitantly as she reached out to pet Shadow again. "Tono...I just wish that knowing me didn't have to hurt you."

"Hurt me?"

"You should be with Autumn right now."

"We're doing well. There is no reason to concern yourself. In fact, tonight she specifically told me to give you her best."

Brie gave him an unconvincing smile, and then started to cry again.

"What are these tears for?" he asked, smiling tenderly at her.

Looking away, she said with anguish, "I just feel all

I've ever done is hurt you. I hold such sorrow because of it."

He shook his head. "Do you remember when I sang that song to you about *The Dance*?"

"I've never forgotten it. It eats me up inside."

He chuckled softly. "Brie, I do not regret my dance with you, however short it was. You opened my heart to a deeper love I did not know existed."

Her bottom lip trembled. "But I broke that beautiful heart…"

"You bruised it, you did not break it. How can I fault you for following your destiny? It allowed me to follow mine."

She glanced at him. "You truly feel that way?"

"I do. There is no need to question it again."

He could see her eyes were still watering.

"Is there something else?"

Her face screwed up adorably as she tried to keep from crying.

"It's okay. You can tell me anything."

"I doubted Sir," she said in the barest of whispers. Brie held her breath to keep in her emotions, and took another sip before speaking again. "Even though he told me he didn't do it. Even though I knew Lilly couldn't be trusted…" She looked into his eyes. "I needed to see those pictures as proof."

Tono looked at her questioningly, not understanding where the deep-seated pain was originating from.

Her honey-colored eyes penetrated his soul when she confessed, "I'm not worthy to be his sub anymore."

The weight of those words seemed to fill the room.

Tono noticed that Shadow had been watching Brie intently when she started crying, and now suddenly got up to settle in her lap. Brie just stared down at the cat, her tears falling freely onto his black fur.

"I know you, toriko. There's something you haven't told me. A reason you felt doubt."

She wiped at her tears, nodding. "There was… The night she accused Sir in China, I could tell something bad had happened to her. I knew it in my gut. I still believe something terrible happened. I just don't know what."

"Didn't Sir Davis always tell you to trust your instincts?"

She nodded.

"He does not fault you for it, Brie. He knows your nature as well as I do."

Brie looked at Tono, her eyes void of their normal light. "I'm feeling as if…people would be better off without me."

Tono was reminded of the dream and ordered harshly, "Stop."

She was confused by his command and began to get up, clearly upset.

Shadow jumped from Brie's lap as Tono took her by the wrist to prevent her from leaving. "These thoughts, they are poison."

She just shook her head, obviously drowning in the darkness.

"Wait here," he commanded.

Tono got up and returned with a single strand of jute, settling himself behind her. In slow, meticulous movements, he began to bind her tight. Brie needed to be his captive audience for her to *hear* his words. If he did not break this dark hold on her heart, nothing else would matter.

"I remember the first time I saw you," he began. "Those eyes captivated my soul. Do you remember looking in the mirror back at me that first day?"

She only nodded.

"I was inspired by the joy of your submission. It resonated within me in a way I'd never experienced. I couldn't get enough of you."

Tono pulled the rope tighter, wanting her to be challenged by the constriction. Forcing her to exist in the moment, not allowing her to dwell in her own thoughts.

"Did you know that I imagined you tied up in my rope on that first day? All I dreamed about was connecting with you through the jute, because I knew even then that you were a kindred spirit."

Brie finally spoke. "I remember how kind you were, Tono. Teaching me a lesson with your tea. You were natural about it and it was not humiliating for me."

Tono laughed lightly. "It was a simple issue easily addressed, little slave."

"My first time with the jute was truly magical. Something I will never forget."

He added another knot and wrapped one arm around her, whispering in her ear, "The fact you enjoyed the wax as well was a pleasant surprise."

She smiled, remembering. "You turned me into art."

"And yet, it was not only your submission and joy of the rope that had me captivated. It was your heart for others and your talent behind the camera. I find every aspect of you fascinating."

Brie shook her head.

Tono grabbed her throat and pulled her head back, immobilizing her.

"Yes, everything about you is special to me—your weaknesses and your strengths. I saw you at the beginning of your training—unsure and inexperienced. And I had the honor of watching you grow into the fine woman you've become. Every moment with you is a treasured memory. Even when I watched you turn and offer your collar to another man."

He heard her gasp and held her even tighter, knowing she needed to hear it. "The pain of that moment is eclipsed by the joy I feel now. It is a part of me—of us. Only you and I share and understand that pain. Only you and I know the gratification of maintaining the deep connection we have despite it. It honed me into a stronger man and helped me survive the death of my father and the challenge of my mother. Your love inspired me to pursue Autumn with relentless determination. So you are not allowed to think others would be better off without you."

He let go of her throat.

Brie slowly turned her head toward him, her countenance notably altered. She nodded, taking in his words before she spoke.

"You changed me, Tono. I now face challenges with a simple mantra—'Just Breathe.' I tackle my films with confidence because of your enthusiasm for my work. Your belief in me and your support of me even after the

Collaring—it changed me inside." She smiled slightly, a glimmer of light in her eyes.

Tono returned her smile. "We are good for each other."

"Yes…" she agreed, nodding.

Knowing he had finally reached Brie, Tono began the slow process of unbinding her—a releasing of his hold on her but with the marks of the rope left behind. A perfect representation of their relationship.

He held her afterward, the two swaying slowly in silence.

Suddenly there was a random tapping on the window. They both turned toward the sound, but the darkness of night momentarily kept the source of it a mystery.

Brie was the first to identify the sound. "Oh my gosh, Tono, it's raining outside! It never does that in LA. Want to dance in it with me?"

"Why not?" he replied.

They walked out of the apartment and into the elevator with bare feet. Brie showed him the way in the dark, guiding him behind the building to a lone patch of grass. She then spread her arms out, tilting her head up to the sky as she twirled.

"I love rain!" she cried.

Tono looked up and smiled as the cold droplets splashed onto his face, appreciating the rejuvenating power water possessed.

Brie grabbed his hands and they spun around in a circle, laughing as they got wetter and wetter by the minute.

She finally stopped and threw her arms around him. "I feel like a kid again, thank you."

He looked at her, watching the water drip from her hair, her smile gleaming in the darkness. It was a cherished sight he would hold on to.

"Don't thank me, thank the heavens for this bounty."

She looked up at him, her voice suddenly serious. "Thank you."

Tono understood what she meant without words having to be exchanged, and he embraced her, holding her tight as the rain fell, washing away the remnants of her darkness.

Twisted

Brie shared with Sir Davis all that had happened with Lilly. Tono left them alone, not wanting to intrude on Brie's private conversation.

He took the opportunity to call a few of his colleagues in LA, wanting to take Brie out for the evening to spend time with her friends at a club. It was something she used to do regularly. He'd been told that The Haven was overly crowded these days, and took the advice to try out its smaller sister club, Twisted.

When he returned to the ICU, he found Brie with her headphones on practicing her Italian. Rather than disturb her, he went directly up to Sir Davis's bed.

"I'm planning to take Brie clubbing tonight. I know some of your mutual friends will be attending and feel it would be good for Brie to get out. Naturally, we'll only go as observers."

Tono did not see a change in Sir Davis's heartrate, but felt certain her Master would not oppose Brie visiting the club.

He turned and looked at Brie. It was humorous listening to her practice. Tono was unsure if Brie couldn't produce the sound or if she didn't hear the nuances of the language. She kept repeating the same phrase over and over, then looking at her screen and frowning. Apparently her version of Italian did not match the program's version, and she was making little progress on her lesson.

Still, it was cute and Tono was certain Sir Davis was enjoying her heartfelt attempts.

He motioned to her headphones, and Brie immediately took them off. "Am I too annoying?"

Tono chuckled. "Not at all. I just wanted to let you know that we'll be headed to Twisted tonight for a little rest and relaxation."

Her eyes lit up. "Are you going to do a scene of Kinbaku?"

"No, I thought you and I would just observe this evening."

"Don't deny yourself on my account. You know how much I love watching you work."

"I appreciate your enthusiasm, but I don't want to make Autumn uncomfortable. The separation is enough for her to handle right now."

Brie nodded, saying nothing, but he could read the guilt in her eyes.

"But you know the saying that absence makes the heart grow fonder? Well, it's true in our case."

She smiled, accepting his assurance that things were well—whether or not she actually believed him was another matter.

"Has Autumn watched you work since I filmed Lea's

scene?"

"No, she hasn't observed my work with anyone else, but we have shared one scene together."

Brie's eyes shone with delight. "Oh, that makes me so happy, Tono! When I met Autumn, I just knew she was something special. And remember the day you first met? I was all excited like it was Christmas."

He smiled, thinking back on that day. "I do remember you were a bundle of energy."

"It's like my soul knew."

"I'm fortunate you saw fit to bring us together."

Brie giggled. "I remember when Lea introduced me to Autumn. I thought she was some kind of freak because she was afraid to meet me. And when we did meet, her face was covered up in that veil and all she wanted to do was hide in the shadows." She snorted in laughter. "Then to top it off, she started spouting bad jokes that equaled Lea's… Little did I know how much I would grow to admire her."

"She is an exceptional woman."

"Autumn is your complement, Tono."

He smiled, agreeing with her assertion.

"Do you hear that, Sir?" Brie said, turning toward Sir Davis. "Another couple coming together all because you handed me that business card in the tobacco shop. You must be so proud."

Brie winked at Tono before slipping her headphones back on and starting up with her questionable Italian.

Tono asked that Brie dress up for the evening's event. She'd been living in "comfortable" clothes since he'd arrived, and he knew it would help bolster her sense of self to dress differently.

Brie came out wearing a simple but classic white chiffon dress. He noticed her playing with a silver necklace that was connected by two condors which lay underneath her collar.

"Beautiful choice."

She looked down, running her hands over the light material. "The dress was a gift from Sir on our honeymoon. It makes me feel closer to him."

"I think he will be pleased to hear that you wore it tonight."

She looked at him admiringly. "You always look handsome in a kimono."

He tugged on the belt of his black kimono, tightening it. "It was given to me by my father. Funny how you and I think alike in our clothing choice."

"We like to honor those we love," Brie said, smiling up at him.

Tono drove to the other side of the city to the BDSM club. Although the traffic was unusually slow, the extra miles were definitely worth it.

The building was smaller, but Twisted was fashioned after The Haven with theme-based alcoves and a center gathering place. It also had the added feature of a second story with private balconies for observers to watch the various scenes below.

Brie shared with him, "When I've come here in the past and watched from the balcony, I've imagined how amazing it would be if every alcove were showcasing a different master of Kinbaku."

He nodded, liking the idea. "That is a worthy suggestion. I will keep it in mind the next time I visit LA."

"Do you really think you'll come back for a visit?"

"Of course, Brie. My family lives here."

She flashed him a heartfelt smile. "I love you, Tono."

"I love you too," he said, putting his arm around her as they walked over to the closest alcove.

Brie squealed in delight when she saw Baron was scening.

Baron looked up for a moment and grinned at her, winking as he covered the large butt plug he held with slippery lubricant. Brie stood completely transfixed as she watched the Dom slowly ease the challenging toy inside the young sub he was playing with.

Brie's rapt attention caused Tono to wonder if she was remembering her first lesson with Baron. She'd shared how important that encounter had been for her. The Dom's thoughtful handling of her that first night had earned Tono's respect.

Hearing the soft moans of the sub resonated through Tono as he watched. He found himself further aroused when Baron open the girl's legs wide and pressed his hard cock against her glistening pussy.

The audience watched in anticipation as Baron forced her to take his entire length with the challenging plug buried inside her. The girl cried out passionately, filling the club with the sounds of her lustful screams as the Dom sank his shaft in deep.

Tono noticed that Brie's breaths had become shallow

and rapid, indicating her increased state of arousal. He suspected she hadn't had any sexual contact since the night of the crash and he hoped the evening wouldn't prove too much for her.

Brie shifted on her feet several times before whispering, "Baron gave us an interesting wedding gift…"

Tono understood her need for a distraction and guided her away so they could talk freely without interfering the couple scening.

"What was the gift?"

"The card only said *An Opportunity to Teach*. Doesn't that sound mysterious and exciting?" she asked, her eyes sparkling with delight.

Tono glanced back at Baron. "That's a very interesting proposition."

"It is." She leaned closer and lowered her voice. "I've always felt guilty that Sir had to give up his position as Headmaster of the Submissive Training Center. He was extremely talented at guiding his students."

"He also works well with fellow Dominants. I had only the highest respect for him whenever we worked together."

Brie nodded. "Yes, I'm hoping Sir will be able to take Baron up on that offer—whatever it ends up being."

Tono thought it was healthy that Brie was thinking about their future. There was no telling what Sir Davis's condition would be when he woke, but to dwell on negative possibilities was a waste of precious energy and time.

"You will have to let me know how that plays out," he told her.

Captain came up to them and held out his hand to Tono. The man looked casual but distinguished dressed in a tan T-shirt, camouflage pants, army boots, and a dark brown leather eye patch.

"Hello, Tono Nosaka. Good to see you again."

Tono took his hand and shook it firmly. "Likewise, Captain."

Captain turned to Brie. "You are fortunate to have such a dedicated friend."

"I couldn't agree more," Brie replied.

Candy moved in to give her a hug. "I've been worried about you, Brie. It's great to see you looking healthy and rested."

"There's no reason to worry about me," Brie assured her. "Sir's improving every day, and Tono has done an exceptional job of getting me back on track. I'm even working on my documentary again."

Tono noticed that Brie had purposely chosen *not* to mention the situation about Lilly. He was curious if any of the Doms knew, other than Master Anderson and himself. He understood why Brie was keeping silent, but suspected everyone here would freely volunteer their time to ensure her safety. She had only to ask.

"Well done, Nosaka," Captain complimented. "Structure is a healthy remedy for stress."

Candy smiled at Brie. "Has Mary come to visit since she returned to LA?"

Brie furrowed her brow, stating, "I didn't know Mary was back here."

Candy glanced at Captain nervously. He cleared his throat for a moment, then explained to Brie, "Do not be distressed by Miss Wilson's lack of communication. She is not in the right headspace to be of any support to you right now."

"That means…"

Captain held up his hand. "Mrs. Davis, I cannot discuss it with you. Be assured that she is getting the help she requires."

"And Mr. Wallace?"

Captain shook his head.

"Oh no…" Brie cried, clearly devastated by the news.

Captain saw how distraught she was and added, "He is also receiving direction. There is no reason to concern yourself about this. You have enough to occupy your thoughts."

Brie glanced at Tono, her guilt easy for him to read. She'd brought Mary to Denver to care for the Wolf Pup during his recovery after the transplant, believing the two were the perfect match. But Mary was a complicated woman. The Wolf Pup had recently shared with Tono that he was struggling with her. Tono thought it was a shame because it was obvious the boy loved Mary.

Tono also knew Brie would blame herself for the pain she was inflicting.

Thankfully, Celestia came over and interrupted the discussion. "I'm so glad to see you again, Brie!" Celestia gave her a quick hug. "My Master will be pleased to see you're looking so well."

"Where is he?" Brie asked, looking around for him.

"He's scening right now. Would you like to watch?"

Brie looked at Tono, waiting for his approval. It reminded him of their earlier days, and he felt a twinge of déjà vu. He'd forgotten how much he enjoyed the simple dynamic between Dom and submissive.

Tono addressed Captain. "Will you please excuse us?"

"Naturally. My pet and I need to set up for our own scene."

Brie's eyes lit up. "Oh, that will be a special treat to watch."

Captain looked down at her tenderly. "I created the scene with you in mind."

Tilting her head sweetly, Brie confessed, "You have me totally intrigued, Captain."

He only gave her the barest of smiles as they walked away.

Tono wondered how Brie would fare watching Marquis Gray. He knew the power of the man and the attraction she had for his favorite instrument.

"Are you sure you can handle this?" he asked only half-jokingly.

Brie giggled. "If I can't, I know where a towel is."

Tono questioned if he could handle being near Brie when she was aroused, remembering just how strong their chemistry was. With neither of them being sexually active at the moment, there was a mountain of unfulfilled need between them. Tono understood it would have to be remedied before the night was out—but in a way that would honor all parties involved.

They walked up to find Marquis with a woman with beautiful curves he'd bound to a Saint Andrew's cross. Her back was to the audience, showing off the sensual beauty of her bare ass. The Dom held two floggers in his hands and was striking her in time with the music of Mozart.

The woman grunted in pleasure as the floggers rained down in wave after wave.

Tono heard Brie's sharp intake of breath as she observed the erotic scene. When Marquis began slapping the woman's pussy with the leather tools, Brie actually lost her balance for a moment.

Tono took hold of her arm to assist Brie, but immediately let go. The contact only served to make him fully in tune with her level of arousal. He took a step back, creating some distance between them, not wanting to increase his own arousal.

Marquis Gray suddenly stopped and turned, staring straight at Brie. She stood frozen in her spot, caught in his intense gaze. He nodded to her once before returning to his play. Celestia leaned over and told her, "Master was gratified to hear you were coming tonight and hopes to talk to you later."

Brie only nodded, her eyes transfixed on the floggers in motion. She scooted a little closer to Tono and said, "I love the way her skin moves like ripples each time contact is made. It's mesmerizing."

"It is," he agreed, ignoring the allure of her scent.

The music built up to a frenzied crescendo, and Marquis met every beat until the very end. The sub stood quivering in her bindings, her labored breaths filling the alcove now that the music had ended.

Tono noticed Brie bite her bottom lip as she tried to control the raging fire within. Wanting to control his own libido, Tono closed his eyes and thought of Autumn. It did not help in the least as images of diving into the woman's sweet depths took hold.

"Maybe we should check on Captain and Candy," Brie suggested.

He opened his eyes and chuckled. "That is a fine suggestion."

They made their way across the room to the couple. Candy was completely naked, except for a thin pink leather collar. She had a sparkly set of cat ears on her head, and was on the floor in the position of a sitting kitten. It was strangely becoming and made Tono smile. Captain held her leash in his hand.

Brie smiled when she saw them, whispering to Tono, "Captain was my first real experience with pet play. We did not have an easy start, he and I, but I will never forget the intimacy of that night."

Pet play was not something Tono had ever dabbled in. Still, he always found it enlightening to witness the dynamics between couples during various types of scenes.

"Did you enjoy it?" he asked Brie.

She smiled, looking at Captain affectionately. "I certainly ended up enjoying my time with him, but personally I have too many fantasies to limit my kink to just pet play."

Tono chuckled, remaining quiet out of respect for the scene beginning, but thought to himself, *You're certainly a challenge with your wide range of kinky desires, toriko.*

Captain sat down on a leather lounger and commanded, "Come to me, pet."

Candy daintily crawled over to him and looked up expectantly.

Captain took a bowl of milk and placed it at his feet. "Drink."

She moved so that she was directly facing Captain as she leaned down with her perfect little ass in the air. She licked at the white liquid, her gaze never breaking his.

It was erotic to watch, the way she seductively drank the milk, her pink tongue promising her Master greater delights.

Captain watched her with a pleasant smirk on his face. It was easy to tell by the look in his eye that he was proud of his young submissive. "Are you ready to learn a new trick?"

Candy let out a little meow and put her hands together in a feline beg position.

"Very well."

Captain removed the bowl and commanded her to sit between his legs. He then produced a candy fish and showed it to her. "Today you are going to learn to balance this on your pert little nose."

Candy let out an excited mew, her hands pawing the air in a show of excitement for the challenge.

Captain leaned over to balance the fish on the tip of her nose. "Don't let it fall," he told her affectionately.

The small fish started to lean to one side, and as much as Candy tried to compensate, it slid off and fell to the floor.

She looked up at him with big round sorrowful eyes and a pouty bottom lip.

Captain smiled to himself, stating, "It was an acceptable first try. Let's see you do better." He balanced it back on her nose.

Candy held perfectly still, keeping the fish in place.

"Now you're not allowed to move from this pose until I say so," he explained as he reached down and began caressing her small breasts.

Candy mewed softly as he teased and tugged on her nipples.

"Don't move…" he reminded her as he began rolling her left nipple between his thumb and finger.

Candy purred in pleasure and the fish slipped, falling to the floor again.

Captain tsked.

The moment he verbally released her to move, Candy lowered her chin to her front "paws" and looked up at him with her ass in the air in a sexy kitten pose that begged for forgiveness.

"Although you have not succeeded today, you have aroused your Master with your attempts."

Captain kept hold of the leash as he unbuckled his belt and pulled it through the belt loops. He laid it on the arm of the chair and patted his thigh, commanding, "Up."

Climbing onto his lap, Candy wore a huge smile as she lay facing him with her head resting on the arm of the chair and her naked body curled on his lap.

Captain began petting her skin as if it were soft fur. "I want you to remain still as if you were balancing the fish, my pet."

Candy made a cute little meow to state her understanding.

Captain then let his hand go lower as he started to concentrate his attention on the area between her legs. She opened her legs a little wider as he began to explore her pussy, spreading her outer lips open before he began rubbing her wet clit.

Soon Tono heard the sound of her slippery excitement. He took a deep breath, reminding himself not to get too mentally involved with the scene. He looked down at Brie and felt certain she was having similar issues.

Captain became more aggressive in the handling of his sub, thrusting his finger inside as he teased her G-spot, then pulling out to lightly slap her bare mound.

Soon Candy was panting, obviously turned on by his rougher treatment.

Captain changed tactics by picking up his belt. "Does my pet desire to be punished?"

Candy nodded, purring seductively.

He folded the belt, pulling tight on her leash as he delivered the first light smack on her ass. Candy squirmed on his lap but lifted her butt for more.

Captain pinkened both buttocks before laying the belt down and returning his attention to her pussy. He thrust two fingers in and began to milk her G-spot. Candy let out a low, sensuous meow.

"Are you close, pet?" Captain asked gruffly.

She looked up at him and nodded.

"Show them how my pet comes for her Master."

Candy threw her head back and smiled as her body tensed. She trembled in his arms for what seemed like minutes before she finally relaxed and purred. Candy lifted her head and rubbed her cheek against him.

Captain chuckled as he stroked her hair. "Good girl... Now for that pink tongue to fulfill its promise to me."

Candy gracefully left his lap and sat down in a cat position between his legs. Captain undid the button and unzipped his pants, freeing his hard cock for her. He lay back in the lounger, commanding, "Lick me, pet."

This kind of play captured a certain innocence that was appealing. Tono had to admit that watching Candy settle between his legs and purr softly as she gave his shaft long, slow licks was provocative.

Captain let out a groan of manly satisfaction as his sub lovingly licked and sucked his cock.

Tono glanced away, forcing his breath to slow as he emptied his mind. Watching his friends scene together had turned out to be a bigger test of his control than he'd imagined. He had to laugh at himself for being so naive.

"Want to enjoy some fresh air?" he asked Brie.

"Please."

The two headed out to the back for some privacy as they collected themselves.

"That was hot, Tono. I think I liked Captain's scene just as much as Marquis's.

He wiped the sweat from his brow. "I'll admit I was surprised by the potency of both."

"I'm really glad you brought me here, but I have no idea how the heck I'm going to sleep after this."

He laughed. "Yes, I failed to fully appreciate the talent of our friends."

"I really like the setup here at Twisted. Seems more intimate, doesn't it?"

"I do like the smaller size and less crowded venue," Tono agreed.

"I wonder what Marquis wants to talk about."

"Why don't you ask and find out?" a low voice stated.

They both turned to find Marquis Gray standing quietly behind them.

"It is good to see you, Marquis," Brie said, looking like she wanted to hug him but was afraid to ask.

He held out one arm as an invitation and embraced her like a father would. Brie lay her head on his shoulder, taking deep breaths as she took in the energy he offered.

"I have missed you, pearl."

She broke the embrace and looked at him sadly. "I have missed you too. Both you and Celestia."

"Is there still no improvement for Sir Davis?"

"He is improving," she insisted. "He just hasn't woken up yet. But I can tell he's close. Isn't that right, Tono?"

Tono nodded. "His spirit is strong when I enter the room."

"Is there anything else I should be aware of?" Marquis asked, gazing intently into her eyes.

Brie shook her head, but said nothing.

"If there were something I could help with, you would tell me?"

Brie's lips began to form an automatic yes, but the force of his stare made her pause for a moment, and she answered, "If I were free to ask for help—yes."

"Meaning?" Marquis Gray pressed.

"I'm not asking for help."

He raised his eyebrow. "I do not care for that answer."

Tono understood his frustration and explained, "There is a special circumstance that we hope to have resolved soon."

"So you are involved?"

"The authorities are involved," he responded.

Marquis turned back to Brie. "This is a legal matter?"

She shook her head. "I can't say."

Marquis stared hard at Tono. "Master Anderson has been cryptic about it, and now you are being cryptic with me as well."

"Out of necessity."

"I do not have a good feeling about this."

"My hands are tied, Marquis Gray," Brie said apologetically.

"They are not, but maybe they should be," the trainer replied.

To Tono it sounded like Marquis Gray was making a joke, but with his intensity it came off more like a threat.

"Marquis Gray, I appreciate your concern for me, truly I do," Brie said. "However, to protect Sir, I'm required to keep silent."

"I am afraid it will be to your detriment."

Brie frowned.

Tono spoke up. "The situation is being addressed."

Marquis Gray did not appear convinced and told Brie, "If you should ever require my help, do not hesitate."

She nodded. "Thank you, Marquis."

He turned to Tono. "The same goes for you, Tono Nosaka."

Tono gave him a respectful bow.

Marquis Gray looked at Brie again, his eyes softening. "I would like to see your face grace my world more often."

She looked as if she were about to cry.

"I will take my leave. Until we cross paths again, Mrs. Davis," Marquis Gray stated.

Tono put his hand on Brie's back. Instead of heading back inside, he guided her to the parking lot. "Well, Marquis certainly took care of my raging libido."

Brie giggled softly. "He has the power to both create and kill it."

They rode back to the high-rise in silence. Tono didn't want to cause Brie more worry, but he agreed with the respected trainer. The chills he'd felt every time he heard Lilly's name had not dissipated.

They walked into the apartment well after midnight.

"I suggest we call it a night," he told her.

Brie nodded, giving him a friendly hug. "Thanks for an incredible evening."

"You have your friends to thank for that, I was simply acting as your chauffeur."

She smiled, taking his hand. "Seriously, thank you, Tono. Being away from the BDSM community, I forget how much they sustain me."

"I felt the same when I was away."

Brie squeezed his hand. "We've been through a lot, you and I."

"We have."

"So, I'll see you bright and early in the morning to

meet with Mr. Thompson?"

"That's the plan."

They both retired to their rooms. Tono had just closed his eyes when he heard the distinctive buzz of the Magic Wand coming from Brie's bedroom.

He shook his head.

There was nothing else to be done after hearing that, having endured a long night of sexual frustration.

Tono took out the photo of Autumn from his wallet and pulled down his boxers. He imagined Autumn leaning over to kiss him deeply with those pink lips while he stroked his rigid cock. It didn't take long before he clenched his teeth in a satisfyingly hard climax.

They met with Mr. Thompson first thing the next morning.

Brie surprised Tono when they arrived at the office. "Tono, I would like you to come to the meeting with me."

"Won't your lawyer be opposed to that?"

"I don't care. Last night, Marquis made me realize just how foolish I am to keep you in the dark."

If Mr. Thompson was surprised to see Tono enter the room, he didn't show it. The lawyer held out his hand to shake Brie's before shaking his.

He indicated they both should sit. "As you know, this is the last day of the imposed deadline, but we have yet to hear from Miss Meyers since her phone call. The police did recover her phone last night in an alleyway near the hospital."

"So they aren't any nearer to catching her?"

"They've increased their presence, but at this point that is all they can do."

Brie shuddered. "It's like she left the phone as a calling card for me."

"Mrs. Davis, she has not sent over any documentation of the genetic test she claims to have. Therefore, I am left to conclude she has no case against Mr. Davis, and is trying to use scare tactics to convince you to pay. I suspect she'll try something today, but hold your ground. She has nothing to support her accusation."

"And if she goes to the press?" Brie asked.

"We will immediately counter with the breaking of the restraining order, her lack of evidence, and your testimony that she has threatened blackmail."

"I hope it doesn't come to that."

Tono could feel her anxiety rising and asked, "How are you doing, Brie?"

"I feel nauseous, but I'm taking heart that it's almost over—whatever happens."

Mr. Thompson stood up. "Miss Meyers has chosen to play a dangerously foolish game. One that will only succeed in landing her in jail."

Brie stood up to shake his hand. "Thank you for helping me through this. Your dedication to Sir and to me has been invaluable."

"While it's not over yet, serving you has been my distinct pleasure, Mrs. Davis. I deeply appreciate the devotion you've shown to your husband, and I hope he recovers soon."

Tono drove Brie straight to the hospital to be with Sir Davis, knowing that the security staff was on high alert. Lilly would not be able to reach Brie unless she physically came to the hospital, and she would be unable to contact Brie unless she called using a direct line.

While Brie stayed in the ICU with Sir Davis, Tono took the opportunity to make the rounds outside the hospital, hoping to catch a glimpse of the woman. He was unnerved by the fact that he did not feel her presence.

The whole day went by without any incident, so Tono was on extra alert as he took Brie home. Again, the police sent regular patrols through the neighborhood, taking the threat seriously.

Brie was convinced Lilly would leak it to the press and spent the night obsessively watching the television, switching channels constantly, waiting for the news to break.

By midnight, Brie turned to Tono. "Maybe she gave up knowing her goose was cooked."

"Possibly," Tono answered, but neither of them believed it.

"Maybe she got hit by a bus?" Brie joked, but her smile quickly faded.

"There is no telling what has happened. It seems odd she would choose to do nothing, but we will not let our guard down," he promised.

Brie gave Tono a quick peck on the cheek. "Thank you for being my rock and protector today. I wouldn't have made it without you."

"You faced the day bravely on your own."

She shook her head. "I was brave because of you."

Intent

Almost a week had passed with no sightings or contact from Lilly. No one could explain the silence. Tono headed outside again, checking the perimeters of the hospital out of habit, and decided to take the opportunity to call Autumn.

"Still no word?"

"Nothing."

"Ren, I don't understand," Autumn stated. "Why would she make those kinds of threats and then disappear without a trace?"

"Remember, the woman is insane."

"So where does that leave you?"

"I'm not sure. It would be so much easier if we knew where Lilly was."

"I don't like this, not one stinking bit."

"Neither do I. It's like she's tormenting all of us by not doing anything. It is an odd dynamic to find ourselves in."

"Is Sir Davis doing any better?"

"There has been no marked improvement, but he

hasn't had setbacks either."

"How is Brie handling all this?"

"She's getting antsy with each day that passes. Wanting me to go home, but afraid to send me away."

"Well, I would love it if you came home—just saying."

He chuckled. "The moment I feel it's safe to leave Brie, I'm on the first flight back to Denver."

"Fair warning, I'll hold it against you if you don't."

"Then I might not," he teased, "because I want you held against me."

It was her turn to laugh. "Take care, Ren."

"You too, little flower."

"What did you just call me?"

Tono smiled. "You're a rare flower I intend to pluck when I get back."

Autumn giggled. "Oh geez, Ren, now you have me blushing."

Tono stared up at the tall building after he hung up and sighed. When would this hospital no longer be a part of his life? When would Brie finally be allowed to move on from here?

Just as he was just finishing up a response to another model who wanted to do a photo shoot with him, Abby stuck her head in.

"Mr. Nosaka, someone would like to speak with you."

He glanced over at Brie on his way out and chuckled to himself when he saw that she was working on the scene of his rope work with Lea.

Tono headed to the nurse's desk with a light heart. "What's this about?"

"Security wants you to join them in the parking garage. Your vehicle was involved in a hit-and-run and they have a witness."

Tono groaned, hoping the accident hadn't rendered the car undrivable.

He popped his head back into the room to let Brie know. "Hey, I'm headed to the parking garage for a bit. Seems someone hit my car."

Brie frowned. "That's terrible."

He shrugged. "I'm sure it's minor. I'll be back in a bit."

She smiled mischievously, pointing to the computer screen, which showed him twirling a suspended Lea bound in jute.

"Good memories," he replied with a grin. "Maybe you can let me look at the edited piece when I get back."

"Sure thing."

Unfortunately, it took almost an hour to sort things out in the garage. The back fender had been severely bent, causing it to rub against the tire. With the help of one the security guards, he was able to pull it back to make the car temporarily drivable until he could get it back to the rental place.

He'd been talking to an older gentleman who seemed extremely excited about being the only witness to the crime, but the guy couldn't describe the driver and only remembered the color and size of the car involved. Tono was humoring him when he suddenly got an uneasy feeling.

Excusing himself, Tono headed back into the building and became frantic when he entered Sir Davis's room and found Brie missing.

He rushed out, trying not to panic. "Where did she go, Abby?"

"I don't know," she answered, sounding alarmed.

One of the other nurses spoke up. "Somebody called Mrs. Davis on a line here at the nurses' station. I had to take care of a patient and didn't hear the conversation, but I do remember she asked for a pad and paper."

Nurse Abby looked up the phone history and re-dialed the number Brie had answered, but she frowned. "That's really strange, it says the number has been disconnected. Let me page Mrs. Davis on the intercom and see if she answers."

Tono waited several minutes but quickly grew impatient. He went back into the hospital room, searching for any clue that might hint to her whereabouts.

Brie had taken her purse, but the laptop remained where it had been. That meant she'd *purposely* left the hospital, but was planning on returning soon. Without a car, however, she couldn't have gone far.

The sickening feeling in his spirit increased as he scrambled to open the laptop, hoping she'd left a tab open with directions to where she'd gone, but found none.

"Where are you, Brie?" he cried in frustration as he slammed the laptop closed.

Just as Tono was rushing out of the room, he felt the overwhelming impulse to look back. His gaze landed on the tray beside Sir Davis's bed. He rushed over and noticed a notepad and pen. The top page had been ripped off, leaving only a torn section behind. Tono studied the pad closer and saw light indentations on the paper.

Heading directly to the nurse's station, he asked Abby for a pencil. With light strokes he shaded over the entire paper, and the indentations transformed into words.

Ruby's Jewel

"What is Ruby's Jewel?" he asked Abby.

"Oh, it's an old bar just down the street, five blocks down and one to the right. It's been here for years off the main strip."

Tono didn't waste any time waiting for the elevator. He raced down the stairs and out the doors of the hospital. The ominous feeling was smothering him now. He feared his dream was about to become reality and started running even faster, ignoring the ache in his side.

He pulled open the old wooden door of the bar and entered. It took several seconds for his eyes to adjust to the dim lighting. He didn't see Brie sitting at the bar counter, and quickly scanned the room. When he didn't spot her, he started checking the booths individually.

Just as he was beginning to lose hope, he saw her in the corner seated across from an unfamiliar male. He snuck up to listen in on the conversation, believing Lilly was somehow involved and hoped to glean information that he could then pass on to the police.

"…yeah, I was worried you'd be too scared to meet. Lilly Meyers is dangerous, but you already know that."

Brie nodded in answer.

"But I couldn't stand back and let her destroy another person for a mistake *she* made."

"Mistake?"

"Look, I don't have time to explain." The man looked at his watch and turned his head, looking at the back of the bar nervously as if he were expecting Lilly to appear any second.

Tono stared at the man intently, memorizing every detail from his voice, the cut of his hair, the features of his face, down to the type of shoes he was wearing. Anyone associated with Lilly was suspect.

"Who are you again?" Brie asked, sounding a bit confused.

"Reese. You know, like the peanut butter cup." He clinked his glass against hers and took a drink. "But who I am isn't important. It's what I've got."

"You have it on you?"

"The proof of the paternity? Hell yeah, I do, but I left it in the car—just in case." He glanced at the entrance door.

"Thank you…for…doing this."

He clinked her glass again. "Anything to right a wrong." He took a big swig and confessed, "I think I'm in need of more liquid courage. How about you?" He kept glancing at the door anxiously as if he were expecting Lilly. "Fuck, if she knew I was here, who knows what would happen."

"It would be…bad."

"I'm headed to the airport and skipping the country as soon as I hand you the document. Can't take a chance she'll find me once she realizes the document is missing."

"No…"

He held up his glass to her. "So here's to giving a bitch exactly what she deserves."

Brie picked up her glass slowly and clinked it against his. The man winked at Brie as she took another drink.

Something felt very wrong.

Tono approached the table, purposely making his presence known. As soon as Reese saw him, the man's eyes grew wide and he froze mid-drink.

The disquieting feeling suddenly increased exponentially when Tono turned to look at Brie.

She stared at Tono oddly, as if she were disoriented. Her voice slurred when she tried to say his name. "Tonnno?"

Tono glared at the man. "What have you done to her?"

The guy put up his hands in surrender. "Hey, look, I only came to help Mrs. Davis."

Reese glanced at the door nervously, but Tono moved closer to prevent any escape. Out of the corner of his eye, Tono saw Brie sway slightly as if she were about to pass out. Without warning, she fell sideways in the bench seat, banging her head against the edge of the table.

"Brie!" Tono cried, moving to help her.

Reese used the opportunity to make good his escape.

A feeling of foreboding clouded Tono's senses as he held on to Brie, fumbling to get the phone out of his pocket. He watched Reese rush to the door and was horrified when he caught a glimpse of what looked to be Thane's mother on the other side—it had to be Lilly.

Tono dialed and put the phone up to his ear.

"9-1-1, what is the nature of your emergency?"

Tono asked the bartender for the address, and informed the emergency operator that Lilly had been spotted and was still in the area.

Brie made a muffled cry beside him as she struggled to sit up.

"What's wrong with you?" he asked in concern.

Brie couldn't keep focused on him, looking as if she were extremely intoxicated.

Tono yelled at the bartender. "What the hell did you give her to drink?"

"She just asked for ice tea, no sugar."

Tono sniffed her drink and caught a bitter odor. He looked at Brie, realizing now she'd been drugged. "Get me some water!" he ordered as he shouted into the phone to send an ambulance.

Tono forced Brie to drink water while they waited as he held her. "Take big sips of the water. That's it."

"My baby..." Brie mumbled.

Tono felt panic set in as he waited for the paramedics and could only say, "Drink more water, Brie."

Thankfully the ambulance crew arrived quickly, being only blocks away, and the police joined them a few moments later. Tono pointed to her tea, telling them he suspected it had been drugged.

Tono stayed behind to answer questions while Brie was rushed off to the hospital. The entire time, he was haunted by the thought that Brie had had the same disoriented look as Sir Davis had in the pictures. He could only hope the unborn child hadn't been harmed by this.

"Mr. Nosaka, we believe if you hadn't arrived when you did, it's likely Mrs. Davis would have been taken to a second location. There's no telling what might have happened after that." The officer patted him on the back. "You're a hero."

Tono shook his head. "No hero here. I left her alone to take care of—" A horrifying revelation came to him. "Officer Ryan, I was called away by hospital security because my car was involved in a hit-and-run in their parking garage. I'm now beginning to suspect it was a ploy to separate me from Brie so that Reese could make contact and convince her to leave the hospital alone."

"How did you know to come here?"

"She wrote the name of the bar on a piece of paper." Tono shook his head, thinking how close it had been.

The officer replied, "I will speak with hospital security. It's possible there may be surveillance video of the accident. I'm headed there now, would you like a lift?"

"I would. I need to check on Mrs. Davis."

When Tono finally made it to Brie's bedside, he found her fast asleep. Needing to know what was going on, he left her to find the ER doctor in charge.

"Will Mrs. Davis and the baby recover from this?"

"We don't know what the drink was spiked with.

Nothing showed up on the standard drug screen, so I sent her blood to be analyzed. However, she's been treated with activated charcoal and intravenous fluids. We won't know for certain until we get back the test results, but I have every expectation Mrs. Davis will be released in a few hours."

Tono leaned against the wall after the doctor left, the feeling of panic slowly receding.

The first call he made was to Master Anderson.

"How could you let her leave the hospital alone, Nosaka?!"

"Look, I was called away by hospital security. My car was involved in an accident in the parking garage. I had no idea Brie had left the hospital until I returned."

"Was I not clear enough about how dangerous Lilly is?"

"I'm very aware," Tono replied angrily. "However…" The reality of what had almost happened washed over him, and he faltered. "I failed to protect her."

Master Anderson growled his agreement, but after a few moments added, "You shouldn't have left her, but…who would guess Lilly is capable of staging an accident and bringing another person in to do the deed. I've failed to appreciate how cunning the witch is."

"The thing that struck me was how disoriented Brie was when I found her. Reese could have led her outdoors and she would have gone freely."

"Oh hell, that sounds exactly like what happened to Thane in China."

"That's what I'm thinking. Brie's confused expression matched the look on Sir Davis's face in the photos."

"What photos?"

Tono closed his eyes, knowing he had said too much. "Obviously, this is not news I should have shared, but I respect you too much to leave you in the dark if you want me to explain."

"I genuinely appreciate the respect but…I do not need to know."

"Very well."

"Did they catch the witch at least?"

"I have not received any word about Lilly."

"How the hell can she keep eluding the police?"

"She is as astute as Sir Davis—able to think steps ahead of most. I was lulled by her silence, but now I realize she was simply biding her time."

"I now understand why young Brie is deathly afraid of the woman. If you hadn't found her…"

"I must concentrate on what *is* and not dwell on what could have been." With that resolve set in his mind, Tono told Master Anderson, "I need to return to the ER and let the staff know the drug used may be of Chinese origin."

"Hey Nosaka, before you hang up, I just want you to know my anger was misplaced earlier. I would have walked right into that ploy to separate you from Brie. We didn't know. We couldn't have known how devious that woman is."

Tono was not convinced. He'd played right into Lilly's hands—was there really any excuse for that?

To his relief, Brie was awake on his return.

The first words out of her mouth were, "Tono, I shouldn't have left."

He shook his head as he pulled down the railing and sat on the bed, taking her into his arms to hold her, needing the connection. "Why did you?"

She let out a strangled sob. "The man said he had the paternity test that proved Sir's innocence, but he only had a few minutes before he was headed off to the airport to leave the States. I shouldn't have gone, but I was so desperate to clear Sir's name that I'd do anything—and Lilly knew that."

Brie buried her head in his chest. "The man was acting so strange when I got to the bar, all nervous and flighty. He even had me check out the back window to make sure Lilly wasn't outside waiting for him in the parking lot. When I returned, he suddenly became animated, insisting we toast to his victory over her."

Groaning, she explained, "I only took a couple of sips of the tea because it tasted so bitter." She began weeping. "I don't remember much else after that. Everything started getting fuzzy." Brie looked up at him with tears in her eyes. "I don't even remember you being there."

She lay back down on the bed, her face twisted in pain. "My head won't stop pounding."

"I'll get the doctor," Tono told her.

"No, he said it will hurt for a while. Knowing the baby is fine, I can handle it."

Tono looked down at Brie, finding it difficult to breathe. "I'm sorry I failed you."

She opened her eyes. "No, Tono. This wasn't your fault. I knew better than to leave the hospital, but I wanted so badly to end this power Lilly has over us." She looked away from him. "I need to beg for Sir's forgiveness."

"Why?"

Her voice broke when she answered, "I could have lost our baby...this is on me." She stifled another sob. "Sir must be worried because I told him where I was headed when I wrote down the name of the bar."

Tono thought about the pad of paper and suddenly realized something...

"Brie, it's important I go now to let him know what's happened."

"Yes," she agreed. Please tell him the baby is okay and how sorry I am." She covered her eyes with her hands, trying to combat the pounding pain in her head.

Tono left her and rode up the elevator, still numb from the day's events.

As soon as he walked into the room, Tono said, "Sir Davis, Brie is safe." There was a momentary spike on the heart rate monitor. Although Sir Davis stared blankly ahead, it was clear he was aware and obviously relieved to hear Tono's news.

As he approached the bed, Tono explained, "The baby is safe as well, but Brie is still recovering from the effects of being drugged. I promised you I would protect her and I almost failed you both."

He took a moment to collect his thoughts before detailing everything that had happened. Afterward he added, "Thank you for your help, Sir Davis. I would never have found Brie if it weren't for the unexplainable urge I felt to look on the tray table."

He moved in closer and said, "I know it was you."

In Another Life

The test results returned with inconclusive results, but the doctor was certain the chemicals were out of Brie's system and her vitals were normal so she was released into Tono's care.

Although her body had recovered from the trauma, Brie was not okay emotionally. Lilly had succeeded in terrifying her on a level previously unknown. It didn't surprise him when she came to him and asked, "Tono, do you mind sleeping with me tonight? I don't think I can face being alone."

"Let me bring my sleeping mat," Tono answered, grabbing his jute mat from the guest room. He didn't feel comfortable lying on Sir Davis's bed, although he appreciated Brie's need for human contact.

Tono walked in and rolled out the mat on the floor. Noticing the dead flowers on her nightstand once again, he was suddenly struck by how disturbing they were. "Do you mind if I throw these out?"

She glanced at them sadly and nodded her permission.

Tono picked up the vase and nodded to her before leaving the room to toss the flowers out. When he returned, he turned off the lights and lay on the mat. "It's been a long day, Brie. Don't try to think, just get some rest for you and the baby."

He closed his eyes and after a long time he finally heard her steady breathing. It brought him comfort as he fought off the guilt, second-guessing everything that had happened that day.

Partway through the night, Brie woke up screaming.

Tono called out to her, "You are safe here with me."

Rather than going back to sleep, she crawled off the bed and lay down on the mat, curling up beside him. "I don't think I can sleep peacefully without a strong arm around me."

Tono embraced her trembling frame, his heart aching for her. Shadow joined them on the mat, snuggling against her belly.

He kissed the top of Brie's head and whispered, "Go to sleep now, toriko. I will watch over you."

Tono insisted Brie return to the routine they'd established, wanting her to concentrate on the future and not dwell on the horrors of what might have happened. He drove her to the hospital and they spent the day working on their various projects.

"Mrs. Davis?" Abby said, peeking her head in. "There's a gentleman downstairs who wishes to speak to you."

"Who?" Tono asked, suspicious of strangers now.

Abby assured him, "I was informed he works for aviation investigation."

Brie was still leery, so Tono insisted on going with her.

The man stood waiting for Brie in the main lobby of the hospital, holding something in his hand. "Ma'am," he said in a respectful tone, "I came to deliver this."

Brie took the beat-up cell phone from his hands and stared down at it. She said in shock, "It's his."

"Yes. Mr. Davis's phone was found near the beach next to the airport. Unfortunately, it was far enough from the crash site that it wasn't discovered until now."

Brie gazed at the phone in stunned silence before pressing it against her chest.

"It still works," he informed her, "which is why we were able to quickly identify it and return it to you." He looked down at the floor self-consciously. "I know how important something like this is to the family members, which is why I chose to deliver it to you personally."

"Thank you," she whispered.

He nodded curtly. "I hope your husband is doing better."

Brie managed a smile. "He's getting better every day."

"Glad to hear it. I wish you both the best, ma'am."

She stared at the phone as the man walked off, the pain and joy of seeing the familiar item written on her face. "Tono, I'd like a moment alone." She wandered off to a secluded table in the corner and pressed the phone to her ear as the tears started to fall.

Tono watched over her, his heart aching for Brie. Although it hurt now, he knew she would cherish being able to listen to Sir Davis's voice whenever she needed to.

After several minutes, Brie dried her tears and walked over to him with a look of concern. "I've wondered why Rytsar never came after hearing the news. I'm afraid he doesn't know."

She held up the phone so Tono could listen to the message.

"*Moy droog*, why haven't you called me back? I cannot reach *radost moya* and you aren't answering your calls. It is not a funny joke anymore. Call me."

Tono frowned when he was done listening.

"I don't think he ever received the call, Tono." Brie looked utterly bereft as she explained, "Judy offered to call everyone for me after the crash. I wondered why I never heard from Rytsar, and even tried to call once, but I couldn't reach him."

"Why don't you head back upstairs and share the news about the recovered phone with Sir while I remain down here to give Mrs. Reynolds a call and find out what happened."

Brie nodded and disappeared into the elevator. Once the doors had closed and she was safely on her way up, he walked outside to make the call.

"Hello, Mrs. Reynolds. This is Mr. Nosaka. Brie told me that you handled calling all of her friends about Sir Davis's accident."

"Yes, that's right. The sweet girl didn't want to leave

Thane's side, and phones don't seem to work in that ICU, so I offered to call her friends. I just wanted Brie to have one less thing to worry about."

"She was asking me about Rytsar Durov. Were you able to reach him when you called to inform everyone about the crash?"

"What was the name again?"

"Rytsar Durov."

"I'm sure I did, but let me look at my list. I wrote down everyone's name and the exact time I reached them."

After several minutes she came back to the phone, sounding nervous. "Mr. Nosaka, I'm not seeing his name here." She started mumbling to herself, "Oh dear...my husband gave me the names of their friends, and I *distinctly* remember writing it down in my address book because it's so unusual." She paused for a moment. "But I'm not seeing it on my list."

"So it's possible he never received a call?"

"Yes," she answered meekly.

"That's fine. If you could give me the number, I'll call him myself right now."

"Oh my, I'll never forgive myself," she whimpered, searching for the number. "Please ask Brie to forgive me—as well as Mr. Durov."

"These things happen. You were only trying to help in a stressful situation for everyone."

Tono immediately called the Russian's number, but it went straight to voicemail and his mailbox was full.

Returning to the hospital room, he found Brie holding the phone up to Sir's ear as she played back a message. "…have you ever considered role-playing Rhett Butler? I'm watching *Gone with the Wind* right now and thought how fun it would be to get all dressed up in a poofy dress and let you hike my skirt up and spank my frilly ass."

Brie blushed when she saw Tono standing there and quickly put the phone down. "I was so happy hearing his call-back message…" She gazed lovingly at Sir. "I just wanted to share something silly and happy with him that happened before…" she said, glancing around the room for emphasis, "all of this." Brie's lip trembled slightly and she slowly set Sir's cell phone on the tray.

Tono walked over to her and placed his hand on her shoulder, smiling. "There's no need to apologize."

"Were you able to find out about Rytsar?"

He sighed before answering. "You were right. He was never called. A simple mistake Mrs. Reynolds is now beating herself up over. More than likely he's not even aware there was a crash because he lives overseas."

"Oh no…" Brie cried softly. "Rytsar will be so hurt."

"Is there any other way I can reach him? The number I have isn't picking up and I can't leave a message."

Brie frowned. "That's what happened when I called." She stared forlornly at Sir. "Although we've visited several of his homes in Russia, but I don't know the addresses. Rytsar shut down his presence online after he was ratted out to the press." She gave Tono a worried look. "I don't know *how* to reach him."

"I'll find a way," he answered soothingly.

Brie glanced back at Sir and shook her head. "This isn't good, Tono. Rytsar will be very upset to find out Sir is in critical condition and no one told him."

"Let's hope he'll understand. It was an honest mistake. No harm intended."

Brie looked at him dubiously. "Let's hope."

Tono spent the day trying to track down a contact number for Rytsar. All of Sir's friends were in the same boat as Brie, having his phone number, but no physical way to contact him.

It finally occurred to him to call Sir's lawyer, Mr. Thompson. Brie had shared with him that Sir and Rytsar Durov had purchased an island together. Surely that meant the lawyer had a physical address for the man.

Naturally, it wasn't that easy.

"Yes, Mr. Nosaka, I have a physical address you can use. If you want to reach him directly, however, I suggest a telegram."

"Telegram?"

"Trust me, it'll be the best way to reach him."

"Thank you for the suggestion."

Tono had had no idea one could still send a telegram. He googled it, and quickly found a company that could send the message. Although they couldn't guarantee Rytsar Durov would be the one to receive it, they could verify the message was delivered to the address given. It was an impersonal way to receive such disturbing news, but, sadly, it was the only option.

Tono was careful wording the message, knowing the

shock his words would cause.

Rytsar Durov,

Please forgive the lateness of this message. Thane Davis was involved in a plane crash and remains in critical condition. Due to an unfortunate error, you were not contacted until now. Mercifully, he continues to shows signs of improvement.

Sincerely, Ren Nosaka

Tono included his phone number, hoping the Russian would call once he received the news. Knowing there was nothing more to be done, Tono shared with Brie how he'd handled it. When he saw the forlorn look in her eyes, he assured her, "Now that the news has been delivered, there is nothing more we can do."

Brie whimpered, "Poor Rytsar... He's going to be devastated by this."

That night, Tono noticed Brie writing in her fantasy journal. Tono realized after hearing her husband's voice, Brie must have felt inspired to reconnect with him in that intimate way.

Tono knew well the types of fantasies she shared in her journal, and decided it was time to do something similar for Autumn. Joining Brie on the couch, he took out a few pieces of rice paper.

Using a hardback book as a makeshift desk, Tono began penning his letter. He wanted to send Autumn an erotic vision of what he hoped to do with her someday. He trusted that by reading it she would not only become acquainted with his deeper desires, but it might spark newfound desires of her own.

Dear Autumn,

I sit here thinking of you.

I haven't said anything before, but I often think of my future—and those visions include you. Rather than keep them to myself, I want to share one with you now.

In the spirit of openness, I will not be censoring my words or thoughts. Take this as my honest feelings and desires.

I envision our first performance together. After months of practice, you have finally come to a place where you are completely comfortable with your body. Fears of the past no longer ensnare you, and you've agreed to work with me onstage in a scene at one of my exhibitions.

I lead you to the mat, our steps measured and exact. I help you to the floor and, in front of everyone, I take off the prosthetic and lay it to the side.

We are both passionate about exposing the beauty of your naked strength and femininity.

Just as we did in my apartment, I sit down behind you and wrap my arms around your chest as we slowly sway to the music, becoming one in spirit.

When I feel we are both ready, I nod and the lights go down to a romantic glow. The song "Animus Vox" by The Glitch Mob fills the air with its raw, sensual undertones. The electronic music sharply contrasts with the traditional flute music that has been the fare for the evening. It grabs the attention of the audience as it lures them with its seductive spell.

The black light is focused on us as I begin the process of binding you. Your body becoming a canvas for the brightly colored jute I'm slowly covering you in.

Because you and I have been doing this for months, you are able to handle the challenging position I am now composing. This position will force you to concentrate on your body—and on me.

My hands graze over your breasts, lightly brushing against your nipples as I work with the rope. The softness of your sensitive skin moves me. Every touch as sensual for me as it is for you.

The fact I am public with my affections, yet remain private in the execution of it, turns you on. I can feel your excitement and longing. The audience can feel the sexual tension between us and it adds to our performance.

When I am done binding your torso in glowing jute, I pull against the silk of your kimono and artfully expose your breasts to them. This is an act of declaration, not exhibition—affirming your femininity to the world.

I now turn my attention to your thighs. As I bind them tight, I take leisurely passes over your panties. You wear a red thong—and it is wet, my little flower. I plan to make it much wetter before I am done.

You are bound tightly in my jute, each knot intricate and purposeful. I cradle your cheek and lean down to kiss you, pleased by your submission and trust. You are a treasure to me—a prize of immense worth.

I want to make this moment more personal and intimate. I pass the jute under your legs, cinching it tight so that it rests between the valley of your outer lips, pressing against your clit. You moan softly, the provocative contact arousing you to even higher levels.

I pull your head back and kiss you possessively. You are about to fly, my rare flower...

The audience holds its collective breath as I begin slowly lifting you in small increments that are timed with the music. You have become a graceful dancer of air as I begin untying and retying the knots to move you into poses that mimic the dance.

With each new knot, my hands graze over your body, reminding you of my desire.

I twist you in the air and the material of your kimono floats around you, accentuating your beauty. The people are drawn to you, celebrating the powerful grace you represent.

They are in awe, as am I.

Before your muscles start to tremble from the challenge of my rope, I slowly lower you back onto the mat and spend the next few minutes gently unbinding you from the restraint of the jute. I hold you in my arms afterward, rocking you as you continue to float on the residual high created by your flight. The room explodes in applause, touched by your courage and grace.

But I am not done with you yet.

Your total submission and confidence is an aphrodisiac to me, and I must have you. Picking you up, I cradle you in my arms and carry you off the stage, determined to have my way with your body in private, while a new couple readies themselves for the next demonstration.

That is my vision, Autumn. It is the fantasy I hold on to and hope to make a reality someday.

Sincerely, Tono Ren Nosaka

Tono folded the letter and put it in the envelope. With a thin paintbrush he decorated the outside with an orchid—but this was no ordinary orchid. It was unique to her, and someday he planned to explain why to Autumn.

He noticed Brie watching him as he finished the last stroke of his brush.

"I always loved the way you decorated anything that's associated with you," she told him. "It made every item that much more cherished."

"I believe things of worth should be given the proper packaging."

She smiled. "I like that sentiment. Do you know I still have the wax cast you made of my body?"

"Do you?"

"Yes!" Brie got up and went to her bedroom, returning a few moments later with a framed shadow box containing the wax form. "It's too beautiful not to keep. Even Sir agreed and hung it up in our closet for inspiration."

As Tono looked at the wax art, memories of that scene came flooding back. "It perfectly preserves that special moment in our lives."

She looked at it lovingly. "It does. So many good memories."

That night, their innocent conversation about the past played into a vivid dream.

Brie stood before him, holding the silver collar and key in her hands. She took a step toward Tono and the

Wolf Pup. For the briefest of moments, she looked uncertain and stopped…

But when her gaze met his, Brie smiled and continued forward.

That smile widened as she approached. Even his father's cold stare did not deter the girl. With the grace of an angel, she knelt down and bowed her head, holding up the collar and key.

Tono did not hesitate, taking the collar from her hand. "I accept this collar as a symbol of the offering of yourself, and promise to thoughtfully guide and lead you."

He knelt down on one knee beside her and whispered, "I will always love and protect you, *toriko*." He locked the collar into place and grasped the back of her neck, kissing her passionately before standing up again.

Brie looked at him with tears in those big beautiful eyes.

He was overflowing with love for her and stated for all the room to hear, "You will wear this symbol of my ownership as a sign of our commitment to one another."

Brie glowed with inner light as she made her vow. "I accept this symbol of your ownership and will wear it proudly for all to see, Tono."

"And I shall wear this key as a symbol of our commitment," he declared, placing it around his neck.

Looking down at her, he stated proudly, "You now belong to me."

"I now belong to you, Tono."

He picked Brie up and twirled her in the air, ignoring the disapproving glances of his father. One day *Otosama* would understand. Until then he would do whatever it took to foster good relations between the two.

Tono noticed the crushed look on the Wolf Pup's face as Mary tried unsuccessfully to comfort the boy. He would have felt badly, but Tono knew without a shadow of a doubt that Brie did not love the Pup. There was no reason to feel anything but joy in this moment.

Mr. Gallant came over to congratulate them, his smile wider than Tono had ever seen it. It was obvious the teacher felt they were a good match. It helped to waylay the palpable displeasure of his own kin.

His beloved new sub stood beside him, graciously accepting the congratulations and well-wishes of their many friends at The Center. In due time, Marquis Gray came up to add his own.

"Tono Nosaka, you are a lucky man to have collared such a prize this evening."

Tono nodded. "I am well aware."

The trainer turned to Brie. "Miss Bennett, you have surprised me tonight, and I am a man who is rarely surprised by anything." He gave her a slight bow. "May you both be happy now and in the future."

Tono was curious about Marquis Gray's comment. He'd assumed everyone would expect Brie would choose him tonight, despite his father's disapproval. Surely the respected trainer hadn't considered the Wolf Pup to be better suited for Brie.

His wandering thoughts reined in when Sir Davis came over and offered his hand to Tono. "Congratulations, Nosaka. I know Miss Bennett will be happy under your charge."

"She is not only my submissive, Sir Davis, she is my soulmate."

Sir Davis gave him a curt nod.

The Headmaster then turned his attention on Brie. "Miss Bennett, you have chosen a worthy Master to collar you. I wish you much growth and happiness."

The look Brie gave him was poignant. "I will miss you…and this place, Sir. Thank you."

He met her gaze. "I will not forget you, Miss Bennett."

"Nor I you, Sir."

He shook his head once, then smiled. "Well, I'm off to enjoy a night of heavy drinking and debauchery celebrating with my Russian friend. Take care."

Tono watched the Headmaster make his way over to the Wolf Pup. He grasped the boy's shoulder and whispered something in his ear. The Wolf Pup looked over at Brie briefly before nodding. Without another word to anyone, he followed Sir Davis to the elevator.

Mr. and Mrs. Reynolds came up to congratulate Brie. "Thane is always grateful when one of his students finds a good Master, and he has had only wonderful things to say about Mr. Nosaka."

Tono was gratified to hear that Sir Davis thought well enough of him to have mentioned it to his own uncle.

"And you, little lady…" the old man started, wiping away a stray tear, "I will miss you more than I can express. The tobacco shop won't be the same without you."

"Yes, Brie," Mrs. Reynolds piped in, "my poor husband will be lost without you."

"I'm so sorry to leave you like this, Mr. Reynolds."

Mrs. Reynolds answered for him. "Don't you worry, dear. He'll pull himself together and figure something out."

"Feel free to visit the shop any time," Mr. Reynolds added. "It would please me to have your spirit grace the place, even if only for a few minutes."

"I'm sure we can make that happen," Tono replied. He looked over at the elevators and saw the pained expression on Sir Davis's face just as the doors closed.

Tono understood.

He would have had the same expression had Brie chosen differently. Tono was grateful Brie had missed it.

"Shall we dance, toriko?" he asked when the music started up.

"If it pleases you, Tono," Brie answered, fingering her collar lovingly, her smile lighting up the entire room.

As they moved across the floor, Tono leaned down to tell her, "I have a confession, little slave."

"What is it?"

"I would rather be alone with you right now."

She grinned. "Me too."

"Shall we begin this new chapter in our lives with a little Kinbaku?"

"Oh, please..." Brie purred. "You *do* know how to spoil your new submissive."

"If you consider that being spoiled, then you are in for a lifetime of being spoiled rotten, my little slave."

The trip home couldn't happen soon enough as far as Tono was concerned. After making their excuses to his father, he sped through the streets of LA, completely mesmerized by the girl sitting beside him.

Brie was his to love exclusively.

He could just imagine it... Together they would travel the world. While she worked directing her films, he would do Kinbaku demonstrations and commissioned photo shoots. Their careers would combine in harmony, each enhancing the other while allowing them to remain together, exploring the world and each other.

Tono smiled at Brie. "You are the most beautiful sub I've had the pleasure to own."

She giggled. "I bet you say that to all your submissives."

Tono shook his head. "Not so, toriko, because you are the first to wear my collar."

Brie stared at him in shock. "Your first?"

He nodded as he kept his eyes on the road. "I have played with many, it's true, but I never found my soulmate until you."

Brie shook her head in disbelief. "Why didn't you tell me?"

"Depending on how the night went, I wanted to keep the knowledge to myself. I did not want that to factor into your decision."

"Oh Tono, I think you've made me the happiest sub in the entire world!"

He glanced at her with a lustful smile. "I plan to make you even happier shortly."

Brie sighed in contentment. "All week I have agonized about who I would give my collar to. I can't believe how happy I am."

He reached over and ran his hand through her long brown curls. "I'm grateful you didn't let my father stop you."

"Maybe in some ways your father was right. Maybe I won't be a good fit for you."

"Not so. I am up for the challenge you bring, toriko. Do not doubt that."

She leaned into his hand and smiled. "If I am your first collared sub, then that means when we scene together tonight it will be the first time for both of us as official sub and Master." She trembled. "I can't think of anything sexier."

"I have waited a long time for this day. Even now it is hard to believe it's real."

She smiled, her eyes sparkling with joy. "Oh, it's real, Tono. I'm your submissive for as long as you'll have me."

"Forever and a day then," he answered.

Brie giggled and leaned over to kiss him on the cheek.

Her joy fed into his own, making his heart full. He'd never believed he could feel such unrestrained joy until he'd met Brie. The instant connection he'd felt on the first day they met had only increased over time until he was hopelessly and utterly in love with the girl.

She lightly placed her hand on his thigh as he drove. That simple contact highlighted the connection between them—it was easy and comfortable but so incredibly intense.

"I love you, Brianna Bennett."

She laughed in delight. "I love you too, Ren Nosaka."

Tono stared straight ahead at the road with a smile on his lips. His life was about to take a whole new direction.

When he got to his home, he set about lighting the candles for her.

She looked around the room at the numerous orchids he'd gathered. "It looks like you were expecting me to come home with you tonight."

"Hoping is a better word, toriko. I have learned nothing is certain until it happens."

"I must say, I picked quite the romantic Dom based on all these flowers and candles."

"I wanted our first night to be memorable."

"Being here with you is enough, Tono."

He stopped for a moment, his hand hovering over a candle, the flame of the match burning bright. "Agreed, toriko. However, I want you to know how very much I cherish you. Now undress and kneel on the mat for me."

He watched her bare her body before him with graceful movements, before lowering herself to the floor. The woman was his ideal—respectful but confident, beautiful but humble, focused but full of childlike joy. A treasure he now owned because she desired it. Was there anything more alluring than that?

Once he was finished lighting the candles, he undressed in front of her. He was slow and purposeful, wanting her to see the naked body of her Master.

Brie's eyes grew wider and more luminous as she watched. He heard a small moan escape her lips as he sat down, cross-legged, in front of her, his shaft announcing his state of arousal.

Tono held out his hands to her, and she placed hers in his. "We made a public commitment, but now I would like to make a private one."

He felt her tremble and tightened his grip. "Brianna Bennett, I will love and protect you all the days of my life. I will guide and care for you, but I know I will also learn from you, my little slave. You have already shown me a whole new world unknown to me before."

Brie smiled and looked down at their hands. "Ren Nosaka, my Tono, I am honored to wear your collar—to learn and grow under your guidance. You captured my heart the first day we met, you enslaved my desire with your jute, and you have always brought peace to my soul." She gazed into his eyes. "I not only give you my submission, but all that I am."

Tono leaned forward and they sealed their commitment with a passionate kiss.

"And now let me love you, toriko." He picked up the length of jute he'd set out and told her to clasp her hands together. With sure hands, he bound her wrists in beautiful knots. She smiled as she watched his progress.

"Turn."

When Brie turned away from him, he lifted her bound wrists and told her to keep the position as he set out to bind her chest. He leaned toward her ear and whispered, "I know how much the restriction excites you."

Brie nodded, her movements slowing as she gave in to the jute. Tono made sure she was bound tightly, making her breath more shallow before he enveloped her in his embrace and told her to lower her arms. "Breathe with me, toriko…"

Tono closed his own eyes as they became one in spirit.

This connection with her was ethereal and every bit as sensual as making physical love. They stayed like that for quite some time before he slid one hand against her mound. Tono smiled to himself, noting how wet she was.

To know someone intimately on a spiritual level and then to connect in the flesh… His body physically yearned for her, and his soul longed to dive in deeper.

Tono woke with a start, his body drenched in sweat and still aroused by the dream. His heart was pounding in his chest. He laid his head back down on the pillow, forcing himself to breathe slowly as the dream replayed in his head.

A vision of another life.

Although beautiful, it was not his life, and his spirit knew it, even in sleep. He had a different destiny, the die having already been cast in this life.

Tono wandered out of the guest room feeling profoundly sad. For some unknown reason the death of his father was ripping at his chest as if it had just happened yesterday. He walked over to the expansive window that overlooked the city and sat down cross-legged as he stared out the window, lost in thought.

He was unsure if his dream had inspired memories of the loss, but instead of running from the pain, Tono embraced it and allowed the grief to flow.

He was drowning in the sea of loss when he felt Shadow brush up against him. Tono made room for the large black cat as it quietly settled between his legs. The cat was an old soul; Tono had sensed it when he'd first encountered the creature.

He stroked Shadow's soft fur as the tears flowed. The two of them one in their grief.

Otosama was gone.

There would be no more intensive instruction in Kinbaku, no more stolen moments singing karaoke together, and no more chances to sit in silence with his father drinking tea as they contemplated the world.

The finality of it hit Tono and he bowed his head, tears falling onto the black fur of the cat.

Shadow reacted by purring.

The sound was unexpected and somehow consoled him.

"Thank you, Shadow," he choked out.

The cat looked up and narrowed his green eyes in answer before laying his head down on Tono's thigh.

There was comfort sharing his grief with the animal. He looked out over the lighted city for hours until the sun crested the horizon with its light. A new day, a new life...

Whatever the reason fate had seen fit to send him here to care for Brie, it had been kind enough to gift him with this moment of genuine mourning. Tono closed his eyes and sent his thought out to the Universe.

Otosama, I can't get used to life without you. I'm afraid I will never stop missing you until my very last breath.

Shadow rubbed himself against Tono's leg.

"I know you miss your Gannon, too. That is our reality," he told the cat, "but I don't want it to be Brie's."

Tono wiped the wetness from his eyes, feeling refreshed after a night of honest grieving. He lifted Shadow from him before standing up, and went to the kitchen to start on breakfast.

Discharged

When Brie walked into the kitchen, he greeted her with a smile and a plate of food.

"Guess what, Tono? I had another dream last night."

Tono tilted his head questioningly, asking as he placed her food on the table, "What kind of dream?"

"It was abstract. More like feelings and visuals than an actual dream. I just remember candles and flowers and delicious bondage—but the best part was that at the very end…" She beamed at him. "Sir spoke to me."

Tono kept his voice even. "What did he say?"

"Hope." She had tears in her eyes when she answered. "It filled me with such joy that I woke straight up, and I can't stop smiling."

"It sounds like a profound experience."

"It was! I never knew Sir's scavenger hunt for coins would end up having so much meaning to me." Brie held out her hand and showed Tono four gold coins with individual letters stamped on them. "This morning I feel so wonderful I could burst with happiness." She broke out into giggles. "I know it's silly, but I just can't help it."

Tono took the coins from her to study them. "Such a deceptively simple word, but possibly the most powerful one in existence."

Brie nodded. "Yes, you can endure anything as long as you have hope."

He placed the coins back in her hand. "I always knew Sir Davis was a wise man."

She giggled. "Just don't ever let him hear you say that."

"I'll take that under advisement."

"I feel so giddy, Tono. Like something big is going to happen today."

"Giddy is good. I'll take that."

She started stuffing the food into her mouth, grinning at him. It appeared she was anxious to start the day.

Tono chuckled, taking the plate from her. "Why don't you get dressed while I wrap up our breakfast so we can eat it on the way?"

"Deal!" Brie cried, running down the hall.

Whether Sir Davis opened his eyes or not, at least for this moment in time Brie was full of hope and the world seemed a brighter place.

They arrived at the hospital far earlier than normal, but the nursing staff did not seem fazed and greeted them with smiles.

Brie ran into Sir Davis's room, while Tono held back, watching her through the glass as she paused a moment, taking in Sir Davis's still frame, before she started chatting away excitedly.

Tono walked in then, uncertain if she would crumble once she acknowledged that nothing had changed.

She wasn't letting that fact curb her enthusiasm. "Oh, Sir, I heard you loud and clear last night. I have no doubt something miraculous is going to happen today." She took his closed hand and opened it up, placing the coins in his palm and letting his stiff fingers clinch around them. "Hope is what you told me, and it is what I hold on to."

She stared at the monitor and then into his sightless eyes. After several minutes, reality set in and she turned to Tono, looking completely devastated.

Tono held out his arms and embraced her when she buried her head into his chest in sadness. He stroked her hair and spoke words of comfort. "Do not lose your hope, toriko."

There was a scuffle at the nurse's station, and Tono turned in time to see Rytsar Durov come rushing into the room. "Get your hands off her!" he bellowed. "I am the brother. I should be caring for *radost moya*—not you!"

Rystar grabbed Tono by the shirt and smashed his jaw with a wicked uppercut. He felt the explosion in his jaw before his legs gave way and he dropped to the floor.

"Don't hurt him, Rytsar!" Brie screamed from behind him.

She fell to her knees beside him, using her body as a shield. Tono rubbed his jaw, stunned by the turn of events, and looked up at the burly Russian who hovered over him, looking like he wanted a second shot.

Rytsar Durov pointed to his chest and growled like an angry lion. "No one touches *radost moya*—least of all you."

Tono slowly stood up, holding his arm out in self-defense. "You've got this all wrong."

The Russian turned on Brie. "Why didn't you contact me personally the minute the plane went down?"

Brie shook her head. "I'm so sorry, Rytsar. Mrs. Reynolds offered to contact everyone so I didn't know you weren't reached until a few days ago."

"I have been leaving messages on Thane's phone, thinking he was playing some kind of joke on me." His voice caught and he turned to look at Sir Davis. "*Moy droog.*" He stared at Sir Davis, tears coming to his eyes.

Brie squeezed Tono's hand before moving over to the bed. "He still remains in a coma."

"But his eyes."

"They're open but the doctor says he's still unconscious."

Tears ran down his face as he put his hand on Sir Davis's shoulder. "How long you've been suffering, comrade…"

"Rytsar, I've done everything I can think of to keep Sir stimulated and comfortable," Brie assured him.

He turned to her, his voice broken when he asked again, "Why didn't you call?"

"I had no idea you didn't know."

"I would have come as soon as I heard. Surely, you knew that."

Brie looked down, her voice trembling as she confessed, "I've tried so hard to be strong on my own."

"And yet you let this man stand in for me?" Rytsar demanded angrily.

She met his harsh gaze. "I didn't ask him to come. Master Anderson did."

The Russian's eyes narrowed. "Where is that traitor?"

Brie put her hand on Rytsar Durov's beefy shoulder. "You can't be mad at him. He kept me safe before he was involved in the car accident."

Rytsar shook his head. "What are you talking about? What car accident?"

Brie explained, "Master Anderson's truck was totaled, but thankfully he only suffered a broken leg."

Rytsar Durov slammed his fist into his palm. "I will add a few more broken bones."

"No!" she cried. "Master Anderson's been nothing but kind to me." Brie turned to Tono. "Both men have."

The Russian glared harshly at Tono. "You have no business caring for my *radost moya*."

Tono was unsure how to react. It was obvious that the Russian was in shock and harbored deep anger that had nothing to do with him. "I came to protect Brie, nothing more."

"Get out!"

"Rytsar, you don't understand," Brie pleaded.

The Russian snarled again. "Get out of here, Tono Nosaka."

Tono nodded, seeing security rushing toward them to stop the chaos. "It's fine. I will leave."

He quickly turned to Brie, adding, "You stay and explain to Durov what's happened."

"No, Tono. You—"

Tono shook his head. "It's okay, Brie." He left the room to assure the staff that everything was under control. He headed straight to the bathroom to assess the damage to his throbbing jaw.

As he stared in the mirror at his swollen face, a smile slowly curved on his lips. The Russian had done him a favor.

He was now free to leave Brie under Rytsar Durov's care and begin a life with Autumn.

Tono drove to the apartment to begin packing his things, trusting that Rytsar would get Brie safely home.

Shadow sat on his bed, watching Tono's every move as he packed.

"It's time for me to go, but I will miss your presence, Shadow. Even though the Russian coming will seem unruly at first, give him time—he actually has a good heart. The man deserves your sympathy because he just found out his best friend is in critical condition. He'll also have been hit with the news about Lilly by the time you see him. It's going to shake him up and he will not be himself. You may want to keep your distance for a while."

The cat gave a low growl as he stood up and walked over, rubbing against the hand Tono held out.

"I'll be counting on you to comfort Brie in my stead."

The cat moved to his other hand.

"Unfortunately, Sir Davis is not out of the woods yet." Tono frowned in concern as he looked down at the black cat. Shadow sat on his haunches and stared at Tono with unblinking eyes. "I do not want Brie to share our pain."

Tono went back to packing, but stopped to scratch the top of the cat's head. "Durov's ways are not conventional, but I have faith he will subdue the threat Brie faces." He paused his hand for a moment, muttering to himself, "He may be the only man who can at this point." Tono resumed petting the black cat. "If he can take care of Lilly, it will greatly lower Brie's stress. I worry about the baby."

Shadow walked over to Tono's suitcase and stepped into it, settling himself on the folded clothes.

Tono chuckled. "I would take you if I could, but Brie needs you, and your Master desired you to stay here."

They both heard the door open and turned their heads at the same time.

Rytsar Durov bellowed, "Nosaka!"

Tono shook his head, petting the cat one last time. "Remember, Shadow, he has a good heart."

Tono faced the Russian, ready to defend himself if needed.

Instead of another uppercut, Rytsar Durov wrapped him in a tight bear hug, nearly squeezing the life out of him.

Tono struggled to breathe and backed away when the Russian let go.

Rytsar Durov shook his head. "I got on a plane as soon as I received your message about my brother. I have spent this entire time out of my mind with worry and then I find *radost moya* in your arms. It was too much."

Tono caressed his sore jaw. "It was a simple misunderstanding."

Rytsar patted him forcefully on the back. "*Radost moya* explained everything."

"Where is she?"

"She was distraught about you so I immediately came to apologize."

"You left her there alone?" Tono asked, now concerned.

"She is with her husband, as it should be."

"Didn't she tell you what's happened with Sir Davis's half-sister, Lilly?"

"*Nyet.*"

Tono grabbed his keys. "We have to go back—now. I'll explain on the way."

Rytsar Durov seemed unfazed. "Do not fear, my men are there guarding her."

Tono looked at him suspiciously. "Why?"

"I trust no one."

Tono stared at him, shaking his head. "It must be a lonely world you live in."

"It is the only one I know. Now, tell me everything you know about Lilly."

As Tono drove, he explained Brie's encounters with the woman, including the spiked drink and attempted kidnapping.

Rytsar went totally ballistic, hitting the car door with his fist as he screamed, "That *suka!*" He pounded the door again. "How dare she try to hurt *radost moya* and *moye solntse!*"

He started pounding the dashboard relentlessly.

Tono put his hand on the man's shoulder. "This is a

rental. It's already been involved in an accident. I do not need the extra expense."

The Russian took in a deep breath and he put his fists in his lap. "I am sorry. I…" he snarled under his breath, "am very angry right now."

"I understand."

"Why is this woman not locked up?" Rytsar demanded.

"The police have been unable to apprehend her."

"Are they idiots?" he snarled.

Tono took a deep breath, needing the man to fully appreciate the serious threat Lilly posed. "Durov, this woman is every bit as intelligent as Sir Davis. She has bested us all, and Brie is the one who has paid the price each and every time."

"No more!" Rytsar Durov pointed at Tono's foot on the gas pedal. "Can't you go any faster?"

"Rather than risking a speeding ticket, why don't you call Brie and tell her we are both headed back. She won't move until we get there."

The Russian growled but pulled out the phone from his pocket to call her. Tono pretended not to hear the tongue-lashing he gave Brie for keeping the information about Lilly from him.

Poor toriko, Tono thought, *you might not survive your Russian protector.*

When they arrived, hospital security refused to allow Rytsar Durov to enter.

"What is this?" Durov shouted.

Tono put his hand on the man's muscular shoulder. "Violence is not tolerated in this environment. Let me speak with the staff and see what I can do."

Rytsar Durov stood at the entrance with his arms crossed, a look of fury on his face.

"That won't help your case," Tono advised. "Think peaceful thoughts until I return."

The Russian growled under his breath.

Tono went inside and headed upstairs to see Brie first. It was important that she knew he was fine and held no ill will toward the Russian. He passed by two intimidating men who were standing close to the ICU entrance. He had to assume they were Durov's guards. It actually gave Tono solace to know Brie had extra protection, and he nodded at the two men.

"Tono!" Brie cried as soon as she saw him. "Are you okay?" She caressed his swollen jaw, tears in her eyes.

He smiled. "I'm totally fine."

"Rytsar shouldn't have hur—"

Tono shook his head. "He was extremely upset about his best friend. It's understandable."

"You didn't deserve this," she said, her bottom lip trembling as she cradled his sore jaw.

He took her hand from his face and kissed it. "There is no reason to be upset. Durov has come to care for you, allowing me to go back to Denver."

Brie nodded, her lip still trembling.

"The only issue is that he's not allowed to enter the hospital. Do you want to help me remedy that?"

"Yes," she said, finally smiling.

They spent the next hour talking to Abby and eventually the administration of the hospital before the ban against the Russian was lifted.

Tono walked outside with Brie to give Durov the good news, and found him standing in the exact same place with the same expression.

"What took you so long?"

"It took some convincing to get them to understand you are not a menace to society," Brie answered.

Durov's frown deepened.

"They've agreed to allow you into the facility but should there be a similar outburst, they will involve the police next time," Tono explained.

Durov snarled. "I won't react unless I am provoked."

Brie put her small hand on Durov's powerful arm. "I need you with me."

His countenance completely changed as he looked down at her and vowed protectively, "I won't leave your side, *radost moya*."

"Thank you."

Tono felt the release of responsibility as he watched the Russian take Brie into his arms and close his eyes as he held the girl. Durov would give his life to protect Brie, Tono had no doubt.

"I promised Autumn that I would head home as soon as I felt I could leave. That time has come."

"Good," Durov stated.

Brie walked over to Tono. He could see she was close to tears, and smiled warmly. "I'm grateful I was able to be here for my family. The next time we meet, it will be to celebrate Sir Davis's recovery."

She nodded, taking a deep breath to hold back her emotions.

"Since I left my vehicle at the apartment, I will I need to head back with you," Durov insisted.

"I'll go with you both then," Brie said. "Just let me say good-bye to Sir first."

Both men followed her up and stood back as she spoke with her husband.

"She's still fragile, Durov. Be gentle with her," Tono said quietly.

"I will honor my brother in my care of *radost moya*."

"Yes, that is what I did."

Durov glanced sideways at him. "*I* am his brother."

Tono smiled to himself at Durov's need to stake his claim over both Sir Davis and Brie, but he said nothing.

Rytsar growled under his breath. "I still need to even things up with that traitor. I will give him a handshake of thanks—with my fist."

"Who?"

"Anderson."

"You do realize he did everything possible to protect Brie."

"No, he did not or I would have been here."

It had never occurred to Tono to question why Master Anderson had asked him to help Brie and not the Russian. However, he could understand why that decision had upset the man beside him. If two men were ever brothers by choice, it was Sir Davis and Durov—there was no question. It was obvious Rytsar cared deeply for Brie and would do everything in his power to protect her.

"I would save your energies for other things," Tono advised him.

"Do you mean my comrade's beast of a sibling?"

"Yes."

Durov faced Tono when he stated in an ominous tone, "She will be sorry she ever touched *radost moya*. When I find her, she will not forget my lesson."

"Don't forget Lilly is pregnant, Durov. The child she carries has done nothing wrong."

"Rest assured, I do not punish the innocent."

Brie approached them with a smile and asked Durov, "Would you like some time alone with him, Rytsar?"

He cleared his throat. "Yes, I would."

She took his large hand and squeezed it. "I think Sir would like that too. We'll head downstairs and you can meet us there when you're done talking to him."

Tono was grateful to have a few minutes alone with Brie. So much had happened in a short amount of time, and soon he would be saying good-bye.

Brie suggested they sit on an outdoor bench, which was covered in warm rays of sunlight.

"I knew he would be hurt, Tono," Brie said sadly.

"The worst is over," he assured her. "Now that he's here and has gotten to see that you both are safe, he will be able to adjust."

She reached out and caressed his throbbing jaw. "Will Autumn be able to forgive me, you think?"

Tono smirked. "I'm sure she'll find my new look rugged and sexy."

Brie looked up at him with those soft honey-colored eyes. "I'm glad you are leaving, but I will miss you, Tono."

"I wouldn't be able to fly out if I didn't believe you

were in good hands."

She smiled. "And I am."

"I'm truly grateful for the time we had. I think it was beneficial to us both."

"It was," she agreed, trying desperately not to cry.

"No tears."

She nodded and took a deep breath before saying, "I plan to keep the routine we've set so I can finish my documentary."

"Good. I'd be honored to see it when it's complete."

"Tono…"

He could tell she was struggling with her words, so he kept silent as he gazed into her eyes.

"Thank you for helping me through this."

"May you never know such darkness again. But you are strong, and you are not alone. Don't forget that."

She nodded.

"You are not a burden—ever."

Tears started to fall, so she quickly turned away. When she had successfully vanquished them, she faced him again, her cheeks wet despite her smile. "Truly, you and Autumn deserve the happiness you can give each other. Your joy is my joy, so please don't be afraid to share it with me, no matter what's going on here."

"I promise."

Rytsar Durov came bursting out of the hospital and announced, "The time has come to make right what is wrong." His expression changed to one of respect when he addressed Tono. "But first we send you off properly, Tono Nosaka."

It turned out that the Russian's idea of a proper

send-off consisted of being escorted to a private jet by his entourage of men as soon as he had his suitcase in hand. Tono had no complaints, however, because it meant he'd be back in Denver and able to surprise Autumn that much sooner.

"May we meet again under good circumstances," Rytsar Durov said, shaking his hand formally as they stood beside the jet.

"And may it be soon," Tono replied.

He turned to Brie then and held out his hand to her. "Until we meet again, Mrs. Davis."

Brie shook it, but quickly broke the handshake to give him a hug. "Good-bye, Tono. Thank you for resetting my course."

Tono walked onto the plane and turned back once. He stood entranced for a moment as a vision of the cherry blossoms swirled around Brie before disappearing up into the sky.

Peace to you, toriko, he thought as he waved good-bye.

Making His Claim

Tono did not call Autumn to let her know he was returning to Denver. Instead, he went straight home to don a formal suit before he surprised her in person.

He was touched to find Lea in the garden singing to the plants while she weeded in a pink bikini.

"Hello, Ms. Taylor."

Lea screamed and turned around, her hand on her chest as she gasped for air. "You scared the bejeebies out of me!"

"I'm sorry," he said chuckling. "I only wanted to let you know I was here."

She stood up, her large boobs making an impressive sight as she tried to slow her breathing. "Wow, what the heck happened to you?"

"A burly Russian."

Lea's eyes grew wide. "Is Rytsar here in the US?"

"Yes, he arrived this morning unannounced."

"Holy moly…" she gasped.

"As you can tell, he wasn't happy to see me," Tono

said, rubbing his jaw for emphasis.

"What's his beef against you?"

"Seems the man never knew what happened to Sir Davis and took his frustrations out on me."

"Oh man, Tono, that looks like it really hurts. Do you want me to get you some ice?"

"No, it looks worse than it feels."

Lea shivered. "Well, he *is* the master of pain."

Tono raised an eyebrow. "Do you know him personally, Ms. Taylor?"

Lea squeaked. "Time for a joke and I've got the perfect one! A sadist, a masochist, and a zoophile were all sitting on a bench at a BDSM club feeling bored. 'Let's have sex with a cat,' the zoophile suggested. The sadist thought about it and said, 'Let's have sex with a cat and then torture it to within an inch of its life.' There was a moment of silence and then the masochist said, 'Meow.'"

"That was particularly awful."

"Awfully good!" she insisted with a grin.

"I hate to think what Autumn has in store for me after spending weeks exchanging jokes with you."

"Oh, I gave her some doozies."

"I bet."

"So how's Brie?"

"She is doing much better."

"Oh, thank goodness! That's such a load off my mind."

He left out the "minor" fact that Lilly had attempted to kidnap her. Mr. Thompson had been able to keep news of it suppressed with the hope that no one else would know the terrors Brie had been subjected to by

Thane's own blood.

Tono shifted on his feet, deciding to get to the point without further ado. "Not to sound rude or ungrateful, but I was wondering if Autumn and I could have the house to ourselves tonight."

Lea pressed her hands together in excitement, inadvertently accentuating her cleavage. "Oh, I don't mind at all. When I think of the look on Autumn's face when she sees you… Oh gosh, Tono, it's going to be beautiful. I wish I could be there."

"So you're fine with clearing out tonight?"

"Not a problem. I'll just grab my stuff and clean up a bit before I go."

"No need to go to any trouble."

Lea shrugged, smiling. "It's no trouble at all."

"Great." Tono was about to leave to get changed, but something had struck him when he'd mentioned the Russian and he felt compelled to ask again, "So *do* you know Rytsar Durov?"

Lea had been trying hard to keep it to herself, but her emotions got the best of her and she blurted, "I totally messed everything up at the wedding."

"How so?"

"He offered to scene with me at the breakfast the morning after…and I took him up on it."

"Was he unkind to you?" Tono asked, suddenly concerned for Lea.

"Oh no, nothing like that. Far from it. It was the best time I've ever had with a man."

Tono curbed his unfounded anger and asked, "What is the problem then?"

"I kinda have a thing for Ms. Clark."

"A thing?"

"Well, it's more than a thing. I've loved her for years, but she's never made a move to collar me. I knew the history between them, but I couldn't resist his charms."

Tono was now beginning to grasp the seriousness of the situation. "Was Rytsar Durov aware of this?" he asked, ready to step in if Lea had been wronged by the man.

Lea shook her head. "No, Brie told me never to talk about Ms. Clark around him. He had no idea."

A new understanding flooded over him. "So you are the one at fault?"

"I just needed to feel wanted, and he wanted me in the most deliciously animalistic way…"

"Does Ms. Clark know?"

She nodded, looking down in shame. "I told her. I didn't want her to hear it from anyone else."

"And Durov?"

"I haven't spoken to him since Italy."

Tono sighed. "So this is the reason you've remained in Denver?"

"I need to make it up to Ms. Clark somehow. I told her I'll do whatever she asks as penance."

"What was her response?"

"Nothing," Lea said meekly.

"Then she has given you her answer."

Lea looked completely crushed. "Please don't say that. There must be a way to make amends for my mistake. I don't care how long it takes."

"If you have asked for forgiveness and it has not

been granted, you must move on." Tono added tenderly, knowing the truth would hurt Lea. "To remain only causes her pain."

Lea let out a strangled sob.

Tono place his hand on her cheek and forced her to look at him. "True forgiveness can only be granted if it is freely offered. When it is forced, it becomes an ugly thing that eventually becomes toxic."

"So you are saying there is nothing I can do to mend what I've broken?" she whimpered.

"I suggest you pour your heart in a letter so there can be no mistake about how you feel and leave it behind when you go. If there comes a day when she can forgive you, she will."

"Oh Tono, I don't know if I am brave enough to do that," Lea confessed with tears rolling down her cheeks. "I've loved her for so long."

"You are brave enough to face the consequences of your choices. Write the letter, then let it go and move forward. To stay will only eat you up inside until you are bitter and hard."

"Please tell me there is something else I can do. There has to be!"

"Yes, you need to let the Russian know. You have put him in an unfair position without his knowledge or consent."

Lea let out a long moan. "Oh God, not that too…"

"Your character and your sanity are at stake. However, it's up to you what you decide to do with them. Choose wisely."

She gave him a lopsided grin. "I have a love/hate

relationship with your wisdom, Tono Nosaka."

He took her hand and squeezed it gently. "Now, Ms. Taylor, I apologize, but I must get ready for Autumn. We won't be back for a few hours, so there's no need to rush."

Lea's face instantly brightened up. "I'm glad at least one of us two girls will know what it's like to be swept off her feet."

Tono smirked at her comment, knowing the plans he already had for the little skater.

When he came out of his room, Tono found Lea busy writing the letter. She looked up and whistled. "You look so hot, Tono. Autumn is going to totally flip."

"Tonight will be a special night. I thought it only appropriate to dress for the occasion."

She leaned her chin against her hands and sighed wistfully. "I wish someone would feel that way about me."

"Patience, Ms. Taylor. Your day will come."

She shrugged, looking down at her paper. "I figured I'd get it over with or I would keep stalling until I convinced myself not to."

Tono nodded. "Wise move. Think of it as clearing the path for your true partner to enter your life."

Lea put the pen down and smiled at him. "Tono, I hope tonight is everything you planned."

He bowed slightly to her. "Thank you, Ms. Taylor."

"But before you go, there's one thing I need to do," she said, getting up and rushing out of the room. Lea returned a few minutes later holding a bunch of makeup in her hands. "You don't want your jaw taking away from the romance of the evening."

She directed him to sit as she meticulously covered the bruised area and finished with some kind of powder to set it. "There!" she announced when she was done. "Still sexily rugged, but not quite so shocking to the eye."

Lea handed him a mirror so he could admire her work. "Nicely done," Tono said, looking into the reflection. "A definite improvement, Ms. Taylor."

Tono drove straight to Autumn's office. He walked in and, with the receptionist's permission, headed over to her desk unannounced.

"Autumn," he called out as he approached her.

She looked up, and her jaw dropped. "Ren? What...what are you doing here?"

"I've come for you."

She smiled nervously, glancing around the office as a blush crept over her cheeks.

Tono held out his hand to her. Autumn slowly rose from her chair and grasped it.

Sweeping her off her feet, Tono cradled Autumn in his arms as he kissed her passionately on the lips. He carried her toward the door to the enthusiastic applause of the office staff.

Autumn stared up at him in wonder, saying nothing as she gazed into his eyes.

Tono felt a rush of emotion and desire. "You've never looked as beautiful as you do right now."

"And you are incredibly hands—" Her eyes flashed with concern when she noticed his swollen jaw. "What happened?"

He smiled as he pushed through the doors and carried her out to his car. "It was a parting gift from a passionate Russian."

"Why would he do that to you?"

"A simple misunderstanding."

"Shame on him!"

Tono grinned in amusement. "I hold him no ill will. He sent me home on his private jet."

Autumn leaned up and gave the tender area a light kiss. "Well, he better not touch your handsome face again."

Tono chuckled, setting her down next to his sports car. "I want to steal you for the day. Is that a problem?"

She pulled her phone out and fiddled with it for a moment. "There, I'm officially out of the office for the day." She looked up at him with a glint in her eye. "Now tell me about these plans of yours…"

"It starts with a little romance."

Her cheeks blushed a rosy pink. "Well, I think you've already got that covered."

He opened the passenger door and helped her inside. "I wanted to surprise you."

She giggled. "I will never forget it, and neither will my office mates. I'll be the talk of the watercooler for weeks, I'm sure."

"I hope you didn't mind the attention."

She leaned over and kissed his cheek when he got in. "Not at all, Ren. It was extremely romantic."

As they drove toward the mountains, Autumn asked, "So the fact you're here must mean that Mr. Davis is improving."

"Unfortunately no, but it does mean Brie has someone else to look out for her now."

"So Mr. Davis isn't any better?"

"Outwardly, no. But I sensed his active consciousness and feel confident he will awaken soon."

"I'm thrilled to hear that. As much as I have missed you, I've genuinely been worried about both of them."

"There is still reason to keep them in our thoughts," he said.

"Something else is going on, isn't it?"

He sighed. "I'm not free to talk about it. However, I hold out hope that Rytsar Durov will be able to set things right."

She leaned over and kissed him again. "Well, selfishly I'm tickled you're back."

He smiled. "As am I."

Autumn shook her head as she sat back in the seat. "All that fuss I made about you leaving, but I was worried for nothing."

Autumn hadn't been wrong, Tono thought to himself. The trip had been far more difficult than he'd anticipated. However, he was grateful he'd been able to maintain his connection with Brie without crossing that line. Instead of his feeling for her causing conflicted emotions now, his inner struggle had only emphasized his desire to pursue the woman beside him with ever greater diligence.

A rare flower was worth the extra care needed.

"So where are we headed, Ren?"

"First, I dine you," he answered. "So I'm taking you to an exclusive restaurant, known for its mountain vistas and intimate dining experience."

Tono was determined that by the end of the day, Autumn would know body and spirit just how much he cared for her.

"Strange how life works," she mused. "I started the day headed to work missing you, and now I'm headed to lunch *with* you."

"Life certainly is full of surprises."

Already he could sense a change in Autumn. The time apart seemed to have benefitted her as well. He smiled to himself. Brie would be grateful to know that—she'd been so worried.

During the meal, Autumn looked at him shyly. "So about that letter, Ren…"

"Yes?"

"It was very provocative."

He smiled. "It was meant to be enticing."

"It was definitely that and then some."

"So you weren't offended?"

"Challenged, yes, but not offended."

He put his hand on hers and asked, "What were your thoughts after reading it?"

"At first I was just plain shocked, really. I mean no guy has ever said anything like that to me before. It was so…erotic."

Tono answered with a slight smirk, "I warned you in the letter I would be frank."

"Well…" she took a deep breath, "it wasn't just

frank, it was wickedly hot."

"After you got over your initial shock, what did you think?"

She swallowed hard before answering. "The idea of being in front of people without my prosthetic totally freaks me out."

"More than being publicly tied and suspended?" he asked with interest.

"Well, that…" she giggled, "that's a whole other can of worms."

"So the idea of that doesn't intrigue you?" Tono asked, probing her to gain more insight.

"Now I didn't say that."

A feeling of providence washed over him and his heart started to race. In a calm voice he encouraged, "Go on."

Autumn's eyes grew wider when she confessed, "The power and freedom of not hiding my scars—but actually embracing them—gives me the chills."

He smiled, nodding his head. "You are a very powerful woman, Autumn,"

She looked down at the floor momentarily before gazing back into his eyes. "You make me believe that."

He tightened his grip on her hand. "I only want to celebrate the strength that is already a part of you. It may inspire others."

She took a deep breath. "Ren…it would be amazing to be an inspiration to other people who carry the trauma of losing a limb."

"You would make a beautiful vision of inspiration. I've seen it in my dreams."

She shook her head, blushing. "You…"

"What?" he asked, amused.

"You see more in me than I see in myself."

"I simply see you without any filters."

She started to cry. "You're too much." Autumn got up and moved closer, wrapping her arms around him, whispering, "Thank you."

Tono turned his head and kissed her, pressing his mouth against her supple lips. He felt an inner rush and grabbed her when she tried to move away, kissing her a second time.

She wobbled slightly when she made it back to her seat and sat down. "Your kisses make me weak."

He winked. "Just think what they could do other places."

She fanned herself. "Holy heck, Ren."

"Autumn, would you seriously consider doing a scene in public—at some point?"

Her green eyes held his gaze when she answered. "I would, but only with you. In fact…" She took a deep breath, releasing it slowly. "I have watched Brie's documentary countless times since you left."

He raised an eyebrow, surprised by her confession.

"I am fascinated by the D/s dynamic. What Brie and Lea do, it…excites me on a level I never thought it could. The more I watch the film the more I long to explore such things. Could you…" Taking a quick drink, she asked, "Would you ever consider training me as a submissive?"

She immediately looked down, the rosy hue returning

to her cheeks.

Tono lifted her chin and gazed into her eyes. "That is your honest desire?"

Autumn looked at him earnestly. "I don't want to go to a school. You're the only one I trust to teach me."

He noticed she held her breath as she waited for his answer.

"I would be willing."

She let out her breath. "I was so afraid to ask."

"Why?"

"What if you said no?"

He shook his head. "Silly girl."

Autumn's eyes twinkled with glee.

"You really decided all this since I've been gone?"

She gave him a seductive smile. "After that letter I became intrigued, and the more I listened to Brie's experiences the more certain I became that I wanted to explore that side of myself—with you."

Tono tilted his head. "You can't know the honor I feel having you ask me to be your trainer."

She looked away for a moment, seemingly embarrassed, but she soon faced him again. "Ren, let me be upfront with you."

"Please."

"I don't want to learn the generals of how to be a good submissive. I want to learn how to be a good submissive to *you*."

He sat back in his chair. "Are you hoping for a collar at the end of your lessons?"

"Only if I am worthy."

Tono nodded, taking all of this in, a bit shocked by the turn of events. He had come here to seduce her, and here she was asking to be trained and possibly collared in the future.

"Before you say anything, there is one thing I have to tell you. Something I wish with all my heart that I didn't have to say."

Tono could feel her tension growing and suddenly grew cautious. "What is it, Autumn?"

She looked like she was about to cry. She held up her hand, asking the waiter for another glass of wine before she would answer.

He looked at her with concern. "That bad, is it?"

She only gave him a tight-lipped smile as she took the glass from the waiter. She finished the entire glass before she spoke again. "Ren, my parents are good people."

"I assumed they were. They created you, didn't they?"

Autumn nodded, but then started shaking her head. "God, I wish I didn't have to tell you this…"

"Whatever it is, I can handle it."

She gave him a look of sympathy. "They are racists." Her face crumbled in profound guilt. "I'm so sorry, but they will not accept me dating an Asian man."

Tono chuckled.

"It's no laughing matter, Ren!"

"This would not be the first time I've faced discrimination, Autumn."

"Well, it's killing me inside because I know how

wonderful you are, but the only thing they will see is the color of your skin."

"What is your plan, Autumn? To hide me forever from your parents?"

"Oh, goodness no! I'm too old to play those kind of games. Besides, I will be proud to bring you home as my date. My first serious date—ever. I'm just warning you it is going to get ugly and I don't want you to hate them because of it."

"I have experienced something similar, but the roles were reversed."

She crinkled her brow. "How so?"

"My father did not like the girl I introduced to him and was openly rude to her."

"What happened?"

"His rejection of someone I loved hurt me deeply and caused her to choose someone else."

"Are you hinting that you don't think it can work between us because of my parents?"

He took her hand and held it tightly. "No, not at all. Later on, after my father had time to reflect, he changed his mind about her. Your parents will do the same. The only difference is that I won't allow them to chase me away."

"And if they don't ever change their minds?"

"Then we deal with it. This relationship is about you and me—not them."

She let out a nervous sigh. "I hope you still feel that way after you meet Mom and Pop."

He cupped her chin. "First we concentrate on us, then we will worry about your parents." He kissed her tenderly on the lips for emphasis.

She smiled shyly when she asked, "Ren, I know your father passed away last year, but how do you think your mother is going to react to me?"

Tono kept his pleasant expression but was brutally honest. "We have parted ways. It does not matter what she thinks."

"I'm so sorry to hear that." She looked uncomfortable but hesitantly added, "Please don't mention that to my parents. They believe that you can tell how a man will treat a woman by how he treats his own mother."

"Since she is the one who severed the relationship, I think they would still approve."

"What kind of mother does that?" Autumn protested.

Tono shrugged, having been used to it his whole life. "She and I never understood each other. It was my father who kept us together. Without that bond there was no reason to continue. I'm actually relieved. She required a lot of energy."

Autumn frowned. "I wish I could tell you that my mother would love you like her own."

"I don't need a mother's love. I had my father, and he more than made up for her lack of it."

"Even though he rejected your girlfriend?"

Tono lifted her hand to his lips. "I would thank him if I could. His actions led me to you."

Her breathing became increasingly shallow and rapid. Tono was unsure of the reason, but waited patiently for her to reveal it.

"Ren, I'm ready."

Tono was pleased, knowing exactly what she meant, and immediately signaled for the check.

Chasing Cars

"Shall we head to my place then?"

"Isn't Lea there?"

He shook his head, grinning when he told her, "I went home first and let her know I wanted to spend time alone with you. She readily agreed to leave the house for the night."

"Does anyone else know you're back?

"Only you."

She reached over to hold his hand. "I like this being our little secret, because it means no one will be disturbing us."

He kissed her hand. "The rest of the day to ourselves."

Once they arrived at his new place, Tono got out of the car and moved to the passenger side to open the door for Autumn. He noticed his neighbor walking toward him on the sidewalk and called out a friendly, "Hello."

As soon as she looked up and saw him, the odd woman pressed her hands together in prayer and bowed her head, staring hard at the ground as she passed by in silence.

Not once had the woman responded to any of his attempts to engage her. He was unsure if she was highly religious or if she was afraid of men in general, but decided after this last exchange that he would respect her need to remain aloof.

Tono helped Autumn out of the car and led her to the entrance. When he opened the door, they were greeted to a room full of shining, battery-operated tea lights.

"What is all this?" Tono asked, looking around at the hundred or more flickering lights.

"Lea!" Autumn cried. "It has to be Lea. This is definitely her handiwork."

Tono spied a bottle of sake on the kitchen counter, along with a note. He picked it up and gave it to Autumn to read.

Hello, my dear friends!
I got these to set the mood.
I know the candles are fake and all
but I didn't want to burn down the house!
Romance is in the air...
Love, Lea

Autumn smiled sadly at the note. "Poor Lea is having a rough time right now, and then she goes and does this for us..."

Tono put his arm around her waist. "Sometimes it

soothes the heart to support a friend's happiness. I've learned that truth from experience."

He took the note from her and laid it back on the counter. "Shall we make use of her gift, Autumn?"

She giggled nervously, the reality of what they were about to do was beginning to sink in for her.

To ease Autumn's mind, Tono told her, "I have a song I'd like to share with you," as he walked to the stereo.

"Certainly."

He took off his jacket and tie before he turned on the stereo. "This song holds a lot of meaning for me. Do you mind lying on the floor with me while we listen to it?"

"I'd love that."

He pressed play and walked to her, helping Autumn to lie down on the jute mat. He purposely positioned himself beside her so their heads were in line with their bodies lying opposite of each other.

Tono listened to the melody that had haunted him for years, but now had a new focus.

Autumn smiled when she heard the first few notes. "Hey, I know this song… It's 'Chasing Cars' by Snow Patrol, right?"

Tono nodded his head.

The two lay in silence, staring up at the ceiling as the lyrics filled the room. Would she understand the meaning behind the words—his heart laid bare?

The last words of the song echoed around them: "If I just lay here, would you lie with me and just forget the world?" and then there was silence.

Autumn turned to him and smiled with tears in her eyes. "Yes, Ren, I'll chase cars with you."

The key to his heart that he'd been longing for finally found its home, and clicked into place...

Tono rolled onto his side to gaze down at her. "I love you, Autumn. Not only because I desire your body, but because I love your soul."

Her smile grew wider. "I love your soul too, Ren."

Tono leaned down and kissed her, expressing not only his passion but the yearning to connect with her. Autumn returned his kiss, lifting her head when he broke the embrace.

He kissed her again with even more passion, grazing her lips with his tongue. When she opened her mouth, and offered herself to him, his arousal shot up tenfold. Her sensual invitation caused him to groan, and he claimed those enticing lips.

This time when he broke away, she moaned in desire. "I want you. I want to know what it feels like to have you inside me."

Chills of desire ran down his spine, and he lifted her hands above her head, securing her wrists in one hand. Kissing her again, he let his other hand travel over her body.

Her body writhed under his touch, communicating its need for him.

"Are you sure you're ready?"

She looked up at him amorously. "There is no other man I want to be my first."

Tono stood up and offered his hand to her. "Then let me undress you by the candlelight Lea so graciously provided."

Autumn giggled lightly as she grasped his hand and used his strength to leverage herself off the floor as gracefully as she could.

Tono gently lifted her chin, turning it to the left so he could kiss her neck before he slowly unbuttoned her blouse. He chose to take his time to distract her from her thoughts while he broke down each wall that surrounded her heart.

Autumn sighed softly when he lifted the material of her blouse off her shoulders and let the garment fall to the floor.

"Your skin is so soft…" he complimented.

She closed her eyes as he gave her light kisses down the length of her arm. The goosebumps that rose on her skin let him know her growing level of excitement.

He unbuttoned her slacks next and eased them over her hips, so that they, too, fell to the floor. Holding on to his hand to gain balance, she stepped out of them and kicked her pants away. She then looked up at him with a mixture of fear and anticipation.

That look was an incredible turn-on.

Tono answered her fear by kissing her deeply as he wrapped his arms around her, lightly caressing her back before he unfastened her brassiere. He felt her tremble in his arms as he slid the straps off her shoulders and her bra fluttered to the ground.

He stood back to admire her body before unbuttoning his own shirt and tossing it next to hers. Tono moved back to her, but instead of reaching out to touch her exposed flesh, he cradled her scarred cheek in his hand and said, "Your body is as beautiful as this lovely face."

Tono grasped the back of her neck, pressing her lips against him as they kissed. He explored her mouth with his tongue as she grew used to the sensation of their naked skin touching. He held her in that embrace for several moments before releasing her so that his hands could travel downward.

Autumn's heart beat against his chest as he started to slide her panties down over her hips. Rather than falling to the floor, they got caught on the material of the liner for her prosthetic.

She groaned in embarrassment and was about to say something, but he just smiled as he knelt, easing her panties down to her feet—his head now directly in line with her naked pussy.

Autumn said nothing as he stared, but he could hear her rapid breathing. "Match your breath with mine," he commanded gently as he lightly brushed her mound with his fingers.

"Ren…"

"Breathe," he told her as he leaned forward and kissed her clit gently.

Her gasp filled the room, but she did not move as she obeyed his command to slow her breathing to match his.

Tono remained where he was, lightly kissing her pussy, and smiled when he finally felt her breaths come in sync with his.

Standing up, he kissed her full on the lips before telling her, "Breathtaking…now sit on the couch for me."

Autumn slowly lowered herself onto the couch, her eyes riveted on him.

Tono knelt again and lovingly took off the prosthetic, laying it on the mat. When he went to remove the liner, Autumn tried to stop him. "Please, just leave it."

"No," he said in a quiet, but insistent voice. "I want to make love to your naked body."

She looked nervous as he rolled it down and freed her from its protective embrace.

Tono put his hand on her thigh and opened her legs wider. "There you are, fully exposed to your lover."

When she self-consciously started to close her legs, he stopped her. "Stay as you are."

Tono got up and returned a short time later with a bowl of warm water and a cloth. With tender hands, he washed the stump of her leg, removing the salt and sweat the liner caused. Once her skin was clean, he cradled her scarred leg in his hands and bent down to kiss the end.

She stared at him with eyes round with fear, like the look of a deer caught in the headlights.

"Do you trust me, Autumn?"

She nodded only once, unable to answer as he pressed his lips against her scars. They were hard and unyielding, having carried the weight of her body all these many years. He continued to give feather-light kisses as he smiled up at her.

Her surrender to him was complete.

In a lustful voice, he said, "My rare flower."

The tears in her eyes only highlighted the intense green of them.

Tono slid his hands under her and picked her up in one fluid motion. She instinctively grabbed on to him, surprised by the move.

"I've never been naked in the arms of a man before."

"I find that very alluring. Shall we take it to the bedroom?"

The fear in her eyes was now replaced with longing, and she nodded.

Tono took her to the room and laid her down on his bed. He then finished undressing, watching her reaction when she saw his hard shaft for the first time.

Her breath increased and for a moment they were out of sync, but she slowly returned to their even breathing without being reminded. It was a positive sign.

Tono lay next to her on the bed and trailed his fingers over the feminine curve of her waist and hip. "The female body is an incredible masterpiece."

She giggled sweetly.

His fingers trailed back up, moving to her breasts.

Autumn held her breath when his fingers touched her hardening nipple. His touches were light and exploratory. Acclimating her to his caress while still discovering her unique femininity.

She moaned and began panting heavily. He had to keep reminding himself that this was new to her, because her body was responding hungrily—wanting the connection he promised and it was designed for.

Tono glanced down at her pussy and saw the telltale pinkening of her outer lips. He was certain if he were to slip his finger between those lips it would come back glistening with her natural excitement.

He gazed into her eyes. "Have you ever touched a man?"

Her eyes widened, and she shook her head.

Tono smiled and guided her hand to his cock and closed his eyes, groaning huskily when her fingers made contact.

Autumn hesitated, then she started petting it lightly as if it were an animal. Her lack of experience was charming and had the effect of turning him on even more.

"Get to know the shaft that will christen your entrance."

She bit her bottom lip as she explored with more interest, touching the ridge of his cock before lifting it up to encircle two fingers around it.

"It's so...big."

He chuckled. "Thank you, a man likes to hear that."

She raised her eyebrows. "Well it *is*."

He wrapped her in his arms, crushing her to him.

"I'm excited and afraid," she whispered in his ear.

He kissed her on the lips, and looked at her tenderly. "Concentrate on my love, Autumn."

She gazed into his eyes, hers becoming more expressive as she mentally let go and focused on him.

Tono caressed her breasts and moved to take a nipple in his mouth. She made an adorable squeaking sound, then began moaning softly when he started to suck. It was exhilarating being the first to introduce her body to the many pleasures it had yet to experience.

"I wanted to make love to you during our trip to Italy, and have dreamed of taking you ever since," he said, moving to the other nipple and flicking it with his tongue before sucking again.

Autumn shook her head from side to side, lost in the new sensations.

He began the slow descent to her pussy, feeling her tense the lower he traveled.

Tono spread her thighs wider and settled between

them. "Have you ever looked at yourself?"

"No," Autumn answered with amusement. "Why would I?"

He reached out and stroked her mound. "Because it's beautiful, Autumn."

She blushed, giggling softly.

Tono opened her outer lips and looked at the small opening of her vagina. It was exquisite in its innocence, having never been breached. He took a long lick and heard her cry of surprise.

"Do you like that?"

"I'm not sure, it's strange having you lick me down there."

"Lie back and close your eyes. Concentrate on the sensation, don't think about what I am doing."

She dutifully closed her eyes and put her head back down on the pillow. He waited until her breathing had slowed before he continued licking and kissing her virginal pussy. Every woman tasted unique: some salty, some bitter, and others sweet. Autumn was a mixture, more sweet than salty—a pleasant combination.

Her tense muscles slowly relaxed as she gave in to the sensation his tongue was creating rather than fighting it. She lifted her head and smiled. "It's like French kissing—but a very intimate kind of kiss."

"That it is, and it excites me kissing you like this."

Her smile grew bigger as she laid her head against the pillow and opened her thighs a little more, her silent invitation to continue.

Tono explored the folds of her pussy with his tongue, only teasing her clit with quick licks and gentle kisses. When it finally stood erect, begging him for more focused attention, he settled his lips around it, flicking his tongue.

"Oh!" she cried out in surprise, sitting up. "Whatever you're doing, I like it."

"I thought you might."

Autumn lay back down, grinning to herself.

Tono continued to build up her level of desire by stimulating her clit with both his tongue and finger. When he felt, she was ready, he wiped his mouth and moved back up to her.

While kissing her supple lips, he began exploring her sex with his hand, lightly touching the small opening with his finger. She tensed in reaction to the contact, but he continued kissing her passionately, wanting her to associate the feeling of his touch with her growing desire.

"I'm going to insert my finger inside you," he whispered huskily in her ear.

"Will it hurt?"

"No."

Autumn relaxed against him as she kissed him back, moaning into his mouth when his finger finally breached her opening. He savored the feeling of her warm, slick inner walls. He could only imagine what it must feel like for her and was gentle as he manipulated her clit with his thumb while pushing his finger deeper inside.

Knowing a woman's body well, he slowly made his way to her G-spot. He stimulated it with light movements and was gratified to feel it swell under his concentrated touch.

Autumn began panting, her nipples hard and ripe as a thin sheen of sweat appeared over her skin.

Tono began sucking on her breasts again as he lightly

stroked her G-spot.

"Oh god, I don't know what's happening…"

"Don't fight it," he whispered huskily.

He could feel Autumn consciously pulling away, and distracted her with his tongue in her mouth while he continued stroking her with the same gentle touch.

After several minutes, he felt her entire body begin to stiffen. "That's it," he growled in her ear.

"Ren…" Autumn closed her eyes and cried out softly as her pussy pulsed in gentle waves around his finger.

He kissed her on the cheek as he slowly pulled his finger from her.

Autumn opened her eyes, now luminous with desire. "I want you."

He rolled on top of her, settling between her thighs as he propped himself up with his arms to look down on her face. Then, taking his shaft in one hand, he positioned it against her virginal hole.

"Look at me," he commanded softly.

She gazed up at him.

"Who loves you, Autumn?"

She smiled. "You do, Ren."

Autumn lay back down and kept her gaze locked on his, making no sound as he pushed against her in light rhythmic thrusts. With each movement, he pushed a little harder, wanting the penetration to be gradual and hopefully less painful. The love reflected in Autumn's eyes encouraged him to continue when progress seemed questionable.

The moment her hymen gave way and the head of his cock slipped inside, she gasped.

Tono held still, letting her body adjust to the unfamiliar penetration and the pain it had caused. After several moments, he leaned down and kissed her as he pushed in a little deeper.

She looked at in him in wonder when he broke the kiss. "Although it hurt, it feels so strange and beautiful to having you inside me."

Tono felt a sense of relief knowing he had successfully guided her through. Now he would introduce her to the spiritual connection lovemaking created. Nuzzling her neck, he began slowly thrusting into her tight virginal hole, each stroke opening her up as he sank deeper into her.

Helping her to orgasm first had made her pussy wet and more eager to receive his cock. In all honesty, taking a virgin felt no different physically, but the knowledge that each deepening stroke was reaching new territory was incredibly arousing.

Tono grasped both her thighs in his hands, using the leverage to begin rolling his hips.

He wanted her to know by his grip that he would not be playing favorites when it came to her body. Every part of her was cherished and would be enjoyed equally.

For him, there were no unsightly scars, no missing limb—only Autumn.

Pressing his forehead against hers, he considered her eyes. "I have longed for this connection with you—to look down at your beautiful face with my shaft deep inside you."

Autumn moaned loudly, her breath becoming ragged. "Ren, I want to feel your essence in the deepest part of me."

He groaned, her request leaving him teetering on the

edge.

"I hunger for you, Ren."

Tono threw his head back, steeling his body for the controlled release he desired to give her.

He was conscious of his strokes as he began thrusting at a faster pace. He looked down and met her gaze, wanting that spiritual connection to be part of his climax. When he could take no more, he stilled his body and stared into her soul as his cock released his seed in rhythmic bursts.

A tear fell from her eye as she received his physical love.

Tono gave one final thrust and then kissed her on the lips.

"I love you," she whispered as she wrapped her arms around the back of his neck and lifted herself to kiss him.

He lowered himself onto her, cradling Autumn in his arms, nuzzling her as he left tender kisses down her neck. "Now there are no more barriers between us."

"I am officially woman," she purred contentedly.

"Tonight you gave me the gift of your virginity. Tomorrow we begin your first day of training, and I will ask for the gift of your submission."

"I can't wait."

"Neither can I," he answered gruffly.

Autumn smiled at him, shaking her head. "You know, I was a good girl until you came along."

"You are a *very* good girl," Tono insisted.

He began kissing her neck and slowly moved down to her breasts, his body already beginning to burn with need for her again.

Letting Her Go

After Tono returned Autumn to her apartment the next morning, he headed back home and noticed for the first time that Lea had left her letter behind.

On top of the letter she'd left a sticky note addressed to him:

> *Tono, could you read through this and give it to*
> *Ms. Clark if you deem it worthy?*
> *Thanks, Lea*

He was unsure why Lea would want him to read her personal thoughts, but honored her request. Making a pot of tea, he took a cup outside and sat on the patio, listening to the mountain birds as he read her letter.

Mistress Clark,

There is nothing I can do to right this wrong.

I have struggled for weeks to come up with something, but your continued silence has forced me to realize this cannot be fixed. I can't undo the pain I caused you, but knowing that breaks my heart even more.

I have loved you ever since training, and always held out the hope that one day you would claim me as your submissive and I would wear your collar.

To be honest, I never understood why you held me at arm's length, loving me, but not willing to be loved. All I ever wanted was to freely love the extraordinary woman you are.

You make me feel things I have never felt with another.

Mistress, your touch, your skin, your fragrance, your taste—all of it excites me. But it's been your brutally exacting dominance coupled with your vulnerable heart that made me fall head over heels for you. Our first kiss was magical—the one when you finally expressed your love to me through the caress of your tongue and the pressure of your lips.

The feeling of that kiss still haunts me...

I am not making excuses, but we both know I made my feelings for you very clear, and you shared on several occasions that you had similar feelings for me.

Why did you never let me in?

It hurt me more than you know. Each time you turned my affection away whenever we got too close.

I'm not stupid. I know you talked to Brie and told her to persuade me to return with her to LA. I didn't understand why you would do that, but kept it to myself out of respect for you.

Here's the thing, Mistress Clark. You still look at me the same way. I know your feelings toward me haven't changed.

But, for some reason, your intentions have.

Rather than let me stay here with you and possibly work out a life together, you decided to go behind my back and talk to my best friend about getting rid of me.

Why did you do that?

Why did you feel it was okay to toss me away without any explanation?

Do you understand how much that killed me inside? Realizing you had no respect for the love we shared or the time we'd invested in each other?

In the end, I came to understand that you had no respect for me.

So I went to Italy with my heart shattered, but keeping a smile on my face, still having no idea how I had wronged you.

When Rytsar Durov asked me to scene with him, naturally my first reaction was to decline. I know the history between you.

But he is an insistent man, and I was not prepared for his overpowering dominance. I will not lie. I knew it was wrong when I accepted his invitation and followed him down to the dungeon, but at the time I was totally bewitched by the fact he wanted me—someone actually wanted me.

I have lived with the shame of my decision, knowing I had betrayed you by willingly engaging with him. As much as I didn't want you to ever find out, I also knew that to find out from someone else would be like a second betrayal.

That is the reason I told you. Not because I wanted to "rub it in", dear Mistress, but because you didn't deserve to be hurt twice.

If there was anything I could do, any way I could right this wrong, I would.

But you have remained silent, ignoring my pleas, and now I have finally come to understand that I have done the unforgivable in your eyes.

I hope someday you will find it in your heart to forgive me. I leave you now, not because I want to, but because I don't want to hurt you anymore.

With all my love, Lea

Tono folded up the letter slowly. Truly, Lea had poured her heart out on the paper. How raw she must have felt after writing it. He wished he had been here to give her a hug when she finished.

He did not feel comfortable holding on to these words, and immediately called Ms. Clark to meet.

"Nosaka, are you telling me you're back?" she asked in surprise when she answered the phone.

"Been back since yesterday."

"Does that mean Sir Davis is awake and no one told me?" she asked, sounding upset.

"Unfortunately not. He remains in the same condition."

"Why on earth did you return? Did something happen between you and Brianna?"

"No," he answered firmly, not appreciating the insinuation.

She protested, "No, no... I didn't mean it like that. It's just that—"

"Mrs. Davis is doing well."

"Well enough for you to leave her alone?"

"She's not alone."

"Who's taking care of her then?"

Tono didn't want to upset her more than he had to and answered, "Another Dom offered to step in so I could return to Denver."

"Come on, Nosaka, don't be coy with me. Is there really someone there for her, or is she handling this alone? I have no problem taking your place since our latest training session is nearly over."

Tono was surprised to hear the Domme make such an offer. "I would not lie to you. Brie is being cared for."

"By whom?" she demanded.

There was no other way around it, so he told her. "Rytsar Durov."

"Damn…" she muttered into the phone.

Trying to change the subject, he said, "I did see the flowers you sent Brie."

"Flowers? I sent those ages ago."

"Well, they must have meant something to her." He chose not to tell her that he'd thrown the dead things out.

"Are you sure that Brianna is all right?"

"I would not have left if I wasn't."

"Then what's the reason for the call?"

"I have something to deliver to you."

"From Brianna?"

"No."

"Fine, be cryptic about it. I'm a busy woman, Mr. Nosaka. We can meet at the coffee shop next to the Center if you can be there in twenty."

"I'll be there."

Tono picked up the letter and headed out the door, curious how their encounter would play out.

Exactly twenty minutes later, Ms. Clark walked through the door of the coffee shop. She nodded to him in acknowledgment as she waited in line to get her drink. A half-smile played on her ruby-red lips as she approached him with coffee in hand.

The other men in the shop took notice of her—it was hard not to. She had a confidence that was alluring and a stylish, form-fitting business suit that accentuated her femininity.

"Okay, Nosaka. What's going on?"

"As you may know, Ms. Taylor has been taking care of my home, and she asked me to give you this." He slid the envelope over.

She looked down at it, her lips pursed in a tight line. Rather than take it, she picked up her latte and took a sip. "I hope this is the end of it."

"Are you speaking of Ms. Taylor?"

She closed her eyes, but not before Tono caught the pain reflected in them. "All I ever wanted to do was protect the girl." Ms. Clark opened her eyes and a slow, sad smile crept across her face. "It's like one of those old movies where the boy yells at the wild animal that has become tame. He tries to chase it away, having to break its heart because he wants to protect it." She took another sip, and added, "Yeah, it's been a little like that."

"She told me about the breakfast in Italy."

"Oh God, *that...*" She shook her head. "How can fate be so unkind to me? And now he's back in LA. It seems I shall never be allowed to move past my sins."

Tono chuckled softly. "That's similar to the sentiment Ms. Taylor expressed."

"The irony, Nosaka, is that I hold nothing against her. I understand exactly what happened in Italy and why."

"Then why have you let her suffer?"

"Because she's the wild creature. I need to break the bond and chase her away so she can run free."

Tono noticed the slight tic of the muscles around her mouth, hinting at a flood of emotion she was keeping tightly in check.

"So you're determined to let her go?"

Ms. Clark shook her head. "I'm not the one for her so I must be cruel to be kind."

"She wasn't wrong when she said your feelings run deep."

She looked him straight in the eye. "I love her enough to let her go. How cruelly ironic that Rytsar is the one who finally set Lea free. Nothing I've done has fazed the girl. But her own guilt, *that* has real power."

Ms. Clark looked back down at the letter. "I don't need to read this. I know what it says."

"Keep it with you," Tono advised. "You may have need of it someday."

She picked up the envelope and slipped it in her purse. Taking another drink of her latte, she asked, "So, about Thane. Do you really think he'll recover from this?"

"I do."

Her eyes softened briefly. "For some reason, I believe you and it consoles me."

Tono knew she had a long-standing friendship with Sir Davis, and her concern for him must constantly play on her mind. "Have you thought of visiting him at some point, for your own peace of mind?"

She rolled her eyes. "Great idea. However, with Rytsar back in the picture, that's not a possibility." She muttered under her breath, "Damn it…"

He wondered if part of her reason for offering to help Brie stemmed from her desire to be closer to Sir Davis, even if it was only through a third party. "I'm certain Brie would help you to arrange it once he's out of ICU. You have every right to see him, and I am positive he would appreciate your visit."

Ms. Clark nodded.

Keeping in mind that Master Anderson wanted him to look over The Denver Academy's interests, he asked, "How is the new session going?"

She raised an eyebrow and frowned slightly, letting him know she did not appreciate him checking on her, but she answered in a smooth tone, "Things are well. Naturally there was an adjustment period with so many new staff members having no experience running the school, but as far as the training of the students, it has gone off without a hitch."

Tono bowed his head to her, impressed that she'd been able to maintain the high standards during the transition.

"So on that note, I should be leaving. The last week is always the most demanding."

"Is there anything you wish me to say to Ms. Taylor?"

She shook her head only once, getting up from her seat and walking out without another word, the sound of her high heels clicking dramatically against the hard floor announcing her exit.

Tono had one more personal stop he needed to make before he completed preparations for Autumn's first day under his dominance.

He met with Faelan for lunch, wanting to reconnect with the Pup after hearing about Mary's departure. The boy looked wrecked, the light in his eyes diminished.

"How are you holding up?" Tono asked. It had become his standard first question whenever they met up.

"Been better."

"I heard through the grapevine that Mary has returned to LA."

He wore a look of defeat when he said, "I couldn't stop her."

"Am I to understand that she went back to Captain?"

"No, she's staying somewhere else. Don't know where though."

"What happened?"

Faelan's blue eyes reflected a sea of anguish. "One day she just said she was sorry but she couldn't take it anymore, packed her things—and left."

"Couldn't take what?"

He shook his head. "Couldn't stand the weight of wearing a collar. What the hell?"

"I'm sorry to hear that. I know how hard you've tried

with her."

Faelan's gaze was soul-crushing in its fresh pain, and Tono found himself momentarily drowning in it. "I did everything in my power, Nosaka. I love this girl, warts and all. I thought we had made real progress, but then she just rips my heart out and leaves."

"Brie was told you were getting support of some kind. Is that true?"

"What did Mary say to her?" he demanded.

"Nothing. Mary hasn't even contacted Brie since returning to LA. It was a shock to her to learn Mary was back."

"Mary can't even do right by Brie when she knows the hell Brie's going through. Why does that not surprise me?"

"Captain seems to think it's for the best."

Faelan snarled. "Yeah, Mary has every excuse for not being a good friend, but damn if she doesn't expect them to be there for her when she needs it."

Tono did not want to go down this path with Faelan so he quickly changed the subject. "Who has been there for you through this?"

"I've been talking to Marquis Gray. He helped me through the 'adjustment' of not being chosen by Brie, so it really sucks that he has to walk me through losing Mary now. I guess I'm meant to be a loner for the rest of my fucking life."

"I appreciate how you are feeling right now. I was there myself not too long ago, but you must never lose faith. When you close off the heart, you extinguish the flame that enables love to find you."

"What? You expect me to lay my heart out again after this?" Faelan snarled.

"Not right away."

"It's not worth it," he growled, clawing at his chest. "Can I just say I officially hate love—like I loathe it to the very core of my being."

"You are allowed to hate it. For now."

"I am done," he insisted, growling in frustration. "So…enough about my pathetic existence. How's Brie?"

"She's facing her current situation with determination, but still needs assistance."

"If you're here, who's helping her?"

"Sir's best friend."

"What? The Russian?"

"Yes."

Faelan smiled for the first time. "So is that the reason for the swollen jaw you're sporting there?"

Tono chuckled lightly. "There was a misunderstanding."

"I bet there was…"

He looked at Faelan seriously and said, "I have to admit you've impressed me today."

The Boy threw his head back and laughed. "Hah!"

"No, I'm being serious. Despite what Mary put you through, you haven't once said you wanted to give up on life."

He shrugged. "I really thought Mary was the reason for the second chance I'd been given, but it appears I was wrong. Fuck it."

"So what are your plans now?"

He groaned. "Well, I sure as hell am not staying here.

The only reason I came to Colorado was to die. Only reason I stayed was because of Mary."

"Where then?"

Faelan raised his palms up in defense, stating, "Before you start making assumptions and lecturing me about it, just hear me out."

Tono folded his arms and nodded respectfully.

"I'm going back to LA. Not in some pathetic attempt to win Mary back—that ship has sailed. But I had a decent job in California and the company said they'll hire me back. I also had my groupies at The Haven. I miss the action there. Besides, Marquis offered to let me stay at his place until I find an apartment. Personally, I think he just wants to keep an eye on me to make sure I don't do anything stupid, but hell, I don't mind. There's a still lot I can learn from the man."

Tono looked at the Wolf Pup with a whole new level of respect. "There certainly is a wealth of knowledge there to be tapped."

"Yeah, so I'm packing up my shit, giving my mom a kiss on the cheek, and then I'm blowing this joint."

"I will miss our weekly talks."

Faelan smirked. "Yeah, I will too, Nosaka. For an old man, you're not too bad."

Tono laughed. "You're not so bad yourself, Wolf Pup."

Faelan looked him dead in the eye. "Someday I'm going to lose that annoying nickname. Not because I punched you in the face, but because I earned it."

"I have no doubt it will come to pass," Tono agreed, suddenly coming to the realization Faelan had already outgrown the nickname. He silently vowed never to use it again.

"So you plan on staying here then?"

"Yes, this is where my life is now."

"By 'life' you mean that Day chick?"

"No. I was referring to Miss Autumn."

Faelan snorted. "Okay, okay, you're right. Miss Autumn it is."

"When you come back to Denver for a visit, you'll have a room available at my place should you need it."

"Thanks, Nosaka. I appreciate that. The fact is, you and I have something in common."

"What's that?"

"Your kidneys." Faelan stood up to shake his hand. "I take the fucker with me wherever I go."

Tono chuckled as he shook his hand. "And you better take good care of it. I don't have a spare."

"You do the same, old man," Faelan said with a wink, shaking his hand firmly.

Tono felt only pride as he watched Faelan walk out the door. He was certain the man was destined to do great things in the future.

Kohana

Tono located a small boutique in Colorado Springs that carried handmade kimonos from Japan. He made the long trip to find a suitable ensemble for Autumn. Because she had specifically asked to be trained to his preferences, he wanted her dressed to his standards.

It excited Tono to think of Autumn wearing his silks tonight and was looking for something that not only complemented her green eyes, but harmonized with the color of his own kimono.

He was charmed by the shop the moment he entered. It smelled of Japanese teas and instantly reminded him of quiet moments with his father. The shopkeeper came out from behind the counter to greet him with a bow. "*Kon'nichiwa*, I'm Ms. Cooper. Welcome to my little shop, it's kind of my home away from home," she explained with pride.

"Does that mean you're from Japan?"

She laughed. "Actually no, but I've always been fascinated by the culture and have traveled there on numerous occasions. I can't seem to get enough of Nippon, so I decided to open this shop."

He nodded. "I can understand. I recently visited a city in Italy and experienced the same love for the area."

Her eyes sparkled when she playfully suggested, "Maybe you should set up a shop too."

Tono chuckled. "Maybe in another lifetime. My hands are full enough as it is."

"Oh, what do you do?"

"I'm an artist."

"Ah, and what's your name? Maybe I've heard of you."

"My apologies, I should have introduced myself. I'm Tono Nosaka."

Her countenance suddenly changed the instant she heard his name. Ms. Cooper blushed and bowed low, stating, "It's an honor to meet you."

"The honor is mine," he replied, certain she must know exactly who he was to incite such a response. She continued to blush and bowed several times as he explained what he was looking for. Her reaction was thoroughly charming, and something he'd often experienced in Japan because of the esteem people held for his father—but not here in Colorado. He'd grown used to his anonymity in Denver and found her adoration sweet but slightly disconcerting.

"Let me see if I have what you want in the back. I just had a new shipment come in last night. Please excuse me, Nosakasama," she said with another bow.

"*Dōmo arigato gozaimasu*," he replied, thanking her in his native tongue.

The smile she flashed at him was priceless as she disappeared into the back. Tono looked around her little shop, enjoying the uniquely Japanese items dispersed throughout the clothing shop—from spices and teas to small knickknacks and candy. The woman had chosen well, bringing a taste of Japan to this decidedly western state.

He determined then that he would return with Autumn in the future, curious which items would capture her interest. It would be another way to share a personal side of himself while learning more about the woman based on which things appealed to her senses.

Ms. Cooper came back with a black kimono and asked, "Is this what you had in mind, Nosakasama?"

She held up the black silk to him. Tono ran his fingers down the strip of green silk that lined the collar, appreciating the print on the material that consisted of various shades of emerald-colored leaves accented with small fuchsia flowers. The addition of green would complement Autumn's eyes and the pink matched her lips, but it was the thin gold rope lining the *obi* that made the kimono stunning and unique. "Ms. Cooper, this is exactly what I was looking for."

"Wonderful, Nosakasama," she replied, clearly happy he was pleased.

While she was carefully wrapping the kimono, Tono picked up a pack of *bontan ame*, a candy of his youth that was wrapped in edible rice paper. "I'd like to get this as well."

"Certainly, Nosakasama. My pleasure," she replied, taking it from him. She quickly wrapped the candy in its own special paper and handed him the two packages. After paying for the items, she gave him a respectful bow. "*Kyō wa dōmo arigatōgozaimashita.*"

Tono bowed to her formal good-bye, and repeated her words in English, "Thank you very much for today."

She opened the door for him, gracing him with a radiant smile.

"Until next time, Ms. Cooper," he said as he walked out of her unique little shop devoted to his homeland of Nippon.

Tono returned home and laid out the wrapped kimono on his bed, putting the treat on the kitchen counter. He'd forgotten the excitement of training someone new to BDSM. It had been such a common thing when he was part of the Submissive Training Center, but he hadn't been with an inexperienced submissive since then.

He smiled, thinking of the butterflies Autumn must be feeling as she returned to her home after work and readied herself before traveling to his home.

She had no idea what to expect other than what Brie had recorded on film. Tonight Tono would show Autumn there was so much more to submission than learning a pose or perfecting a sensual skill.

He had just finished dressing in his kimono when he heard a light knock on the door. He was pleased that she was fifteen minutes sooner than expected. It was obvious she had paid close attention to the documentary and understood lateness was considered a sign of disrespect.

Tono opened the door and smiled. "Are you ready for your first lesson, Autumn?"

She gave him a timid, but charming "Yes."

"Excellent. You will come in and go to my room. There you will find the outfit I have chosen for you. Unlike before, you are not allowed to wear any under-garments. I want you naked under the silk."

Autumn caught her breath, surprised to be given or-ders before she had even stepped inside. Tono watched her intently, curious to see how she would handle it. Her response would let him know how serious she was about wanting to be trained.

"What is the proper way to say yes?"

He nodded his approval for her asking. "A simple '*Hai*, Tono' will do. It basically means 'Yes Master'."

"And if I want to respond in the negative?"

"I will keep it simple and let you answer with '*Kamo*, Tono,' which means 'Probably, Master'."

He enjoyed the smirk that played across her lips when she realized when she said no, it was still an affirmative response.

"We will speak more on the subject after you dress."

"*Hai*, Tono," she answered, giving him a shy little bow before heading down the hall to his bedroom.

He stood in the hallway, with his hands behind his back, waiting patiently for her to join him.

"Oh Tono, what a beautiful kimono!" she exclaimed from his bedroom.

"I am pleased that you like it," he replied, smirking to himself.

Autumn took an exceedingly long time putting it on. Finally, she called out, "Tono?"

"Yes, Autumn?"

"I'm sorry, but I can't figure out this belt."

Tono chuckled to himself, but answered in a firm tone, "Come out here, and I will show you how to tie it correctly."

Autumn made her way out of his bedroom with one hand clutched around the *obi* while the other held her kimono closed. Even though they had seen each other completely naked just yesterday, it was apparent that she still struggled with exposing her body to him—but she was too much of a beauty to be kept under wraps.

"Hand me the belt," he commanded, "and go to the mirror, putting your hands out to your sides."

She hesitated for a moment as it dawned on her that to obey his command would leave the kimono open, but she respectfully gave him the sash and walked over to the mirror, lifting her arms out and allowing the kimono to fall open.

Just that brief glance of her naked skin had fire rushing to his groin. Oh, the things he planned to do with her...

Tono forced his thoughts in check and demonstrated how to properly tie the *obi* around her waist. He informed her, "As my submissive, I will call you by a special name."

Autumn turned her head slightly to look at him. "What name, Tono?"

"Pay attention," he admonished with a slight grin, tightening the sash. "I'll tell you once you can tie this yourself."

She quickly turned to look down at his hands as he finished the intricate tie. As soon as he was done, he undid the *obi* and handed it to her.

"Show me what you have learned."

Autumn gave him a doubtful look, but adjusted her kimono and folded the top part of the obi in half and laid it against her shoulder. She got as far as wrapping it around her waist twice before she got confused and was forced to stop.

"Undo it and hand it to me," he commanded.

Tono showed her again and was heartened to see her increased concentration. When he gave it to her the second time, she seemed far more confident.

Although it took her a while, and involved several reties, she finally finished and turned the *hane* to the back before carefully straightening it. When she was done, she looked into the reflection of the mirror and smiled at him.

"I'm impressed," he said with sincerity, "considering I only showed you twice."

Autumn couldn't hide her joy, beaming with pride when she said, "Thank you, Tono."

"Now that you are dressed as my submissive in training, it's time to make this arrangement official."

He turned her around to face him. Gazing into her green eyes, he asked, "Autumn Day, do you consent to train under my care for the next three months?"

"*Hai*, Tono."

He pulled a thin strand of jute fashioned with delicate knots that he had created for this occasion. "While this is not a formal collar, you are not allowed to take it off. It is a reminder of the commitment you are making to me this evening."

Tono tied the jute securely around her neck, looking down at her as he did so. Her eyes were so wide and trusting...

Autumn trailed her fingers over the jute when he was done, a sweet smile on her lips.

He stated formally, "Your name is now kohana."

"Kahawna?" she repeated carefully.

"It is the Japanese word for 'little flower'." He placed his finger under her chin and tilted her head up. "I consider you the rarest of flowers and am honored to be the man to train you."

"Oh Tono..." she whispered, her voice heavy with emotion.

"You are now officially my submissive student. You will only answer to me as your Master."

Autumn nodded. "That is my heart's desire, Tono."

He sealed their commitment with a kiss before turning back to face the mirror.

"Look in the mirror," he commanded gently, standing behind her.

Autumn looked absolutely stunning standing there. The black kimono was sexy, but still hinted to her innocence with the artful placement of the flowers.

"Before you stands a woman on the precipice of a great journey. Are you ready to explore your hidden desires with me?"

"*Hai*, Tono," she answered, her eyes luminous and enchanting as she looked at him in the reflection.

"Come," he said, directing her to the jute mat. After helping her to the floor, he sat cross-legged facing her. "When you arrived, I said that we would talk more about expected protocols. As your Dominant, I must be clear in my instructions. As the submissive it is important that you ask questions if you are unsure, but then immediately obey once the explanation has been given."

He noticed her swallow hard, the reality of this venture hitting home for her.

"If I ask a question and you give a positive response, I know you are fully willing. If you answer with *Kamo*, it lets me know your reluctance. Ultimately, however, as the Dominant my will is to be obeyed. I can choose to amend the command or not. If I choose not to, you are expected to obey despite your stated feelings."

Her eyes grew even wider.

"But if at any point you wish to stop a scene, I expect you to call out your safeword."

"What is my safeword, Tono?"

"*Aka.*"

"What does that mean?"

"The color red."

She nodded. "Yes, I remember the different safewords from the film, so how do you say yellow?"

"*Kiiro.*"

"And green?"

"*Midori.* Now say them for me."

Autumn repeated the three words flawlessly.

"Well done, kohana."

Autumn blushed, obviously pleased by his praise.

"My next task may prove challenging because of your

prosthetic, but I want you to find a comfortable kneeling position you can maintain. Try different poses until you find the one that suits you and is pleasing to the eye. Use the mirror to guide you. In this case, what I desire is a position that expresses your submission to me but is also comfortable."

"I will do my best, Tono," she answered, sounding a tad nervous. He suspected she was afraid of failing in the task, but she would soon learn that his brand of instruction would not set her up for failure, only success.

Tono stood back and watched as Autumn carefully lowered herself to the ground and began experimenting. After trying several different positions, she returned to the first one and announced, "I believe this is the one, Tono."

"It is an extremely attractive pose, but I am going to ask that you stay in that position until I give you permission to move from it. Let's see if it is something you can maintain comfortably for an extended amount of time."

After only a few minutes, he saw her shifting slightly.

"Find another," he commanded.

Autumn frowned, looking as if she were embarrassed to have chosen incorrectly, but dutifully tried several more positions before choosing another.

"Very well. Stay as you are until I tell you otherwise."

"*Hai*, Tono."

He kept her in that pose for over fifteen minutes before he walked up to her. "I appreciate the grace expressed in this pose, but we need to add another element." He knelt down on one knee and pulled at the collar of her kimono, opening it wider until the beauty of

245

her breasts were exposed. He ran his fingers over the soft silk and her smooth skin, communicating his pleasure in her choice with both his touch and his words.

"I like that you hold your hands open, exposing your palms," Tono said as he lightly traced his finger over the sensitive area. Leaning forward, he whispered in her ear, "And your thighs being parted communicates your willingness to satisfy my needs…" He took advantage of the opening of her kimono to slowly run his hand up her inner thigh, stopping just shy of her mound.

He felt her tense in anticipation.

Tono smiled as he removed his hand from her thigh and lightly grazed her bottom lip with his finger instead.

He kissed her then. The kiss started out tender but quickly grew more passionate as Autumn responded when he parted her lips with his tongue. Her soft moans and rapid breath called to him, and he had to fight the overwhelming urge to take her right there on the mat.

Standing up, he walked over to the counter, picking up the *bontan* candy and returning to hand it to her. "A small gift for succeeding in your task. This hints to my childhood."

"Thank you, Tono," she said, eagerly unwrapping the small present. She smiled when she saw what it was. "This is the candy you ate as a boy?"

Tono nodded. "Have you had it before?"

She shook her head.

"It's unique because it is wrapped in rice paper, which is meant to be eaten with the candy."

Autumn opened the small box and handed him one piece before taking one for herself. She studied the clear wrapper encasing the candy. "It looks like plastic. Is it really edible?"

"Not the first wrap." He unwrapped it from the plastic to reveal a small orange candy wrapped in clear rice paper. Tono popped it into his mouth and let the rice paper melt on his tongue before he started chewing the soft citrus candy.

Autumn smiled and unwrapped hers and took a bite into it. She looked confused as she tried to break the paper with her teeth. She put her hand up to cover her mouth and said, "Are you sure it's not plastic?"

Tono opened his mouth and stuck out his tongue to show her the candy was gone.

A smile appeared on Autumn's face when the rice paper began to melt in her mouth. After she chewed and swallowed the candy, she told him, "I can see why you enjoyed it as a kid. Edible paper has to be the funnest thing ever."

She offered him another piece before popping a second one in her mouth.

Tono thoroughly enjoyed sharing this small element of his life with her. The fact she was equally thrilled only helped to endear her to him even more.

"Now that your kneeling position is set and your safewords are established, let's begin with your first lesson."

He noticed Autumn momentarily freeze, a terrified look flitting across her face.

"I am a gentle but exacting teacher, kohana. There is no reason to fear the lessons I teach."

Autumn shook her head. "I'm sorry, Tono. All of

this is so new, I kind of forgot myself for a moment."

"There is an excitement in each new experience with a partner. It will bond the two of us in a unique way."

She blushed. "Yes, I experienced that last night."

The mention of their first coupling caused his cock to harden as thoughts of claiming her virginity rushed back to his mind.

Her recent initiation to full penetration was the reason he was taking it slow with her today. Since this would be only their second time together, he felt a gentle introduction would set her up for a lifetime of exploration.

Autumn was truly a rare treasure as a new submissive. She was a strong, experienced woman and survivor, yet she possessed the innocence of a girl just coming into her own sexually. It was a pleasure to savor and enjoy both aspects of her.

Tono struck a match and lit a large red candle. "Tonight I will be introducing you to wax play."

She nervously glanced at the candle.

Her inexperience was a definite turn-on. To see in her eyes the fear of something she would soon grow to love was intoxicating to him.

"Remove your kimono and sit on the mat, kohana."

She did not hesitate this time, undoing the sash and letting the kimono gently fall to the floor. Before he would let her sit, Tono stared at her, admiring her breasts, bare sex, and those shapely thighs. Autumn glanced down briefly at her prosthetic, frowning slightly before looking away.

He smiled. "Yes, kohana, I see it but it does not detract from your beauty. Do not concern yourself with that again."

She nodded curtly, her unconscious action revealing that she'd heard his words but had not accepted his truth.

That would be a lesson for another day.

Tono sat down behind her with the burning pillar candle in his hand and commanded, "Lean your back against me."

She moved closer to him and leaned her naked body against his chest, the contact sending a sexual current through them both.

"Now this requires that you trust your Master. I want you to stay still."

"*Hai*, Tono," she said in a breathless voice.

He grasped her throat with his free hand and forced her head back so her lips were accessible to him.

"Trust…" he murmured huskily as he tipped the candle and the first drops fell. She twitched when the hot wax made contact with her skin, leaving trails of red following the valley between her breasts.

"Color?"

She giggled. "*Midori*, Tono. I actually liked it."

"Now that you are familiar with its warm caress, I want you to stay still this time."

"I'm sorry I flinched."

"It was an involuntary reflex and not a conscious choice to move. Had it been not so, I would punish you for willful disobedience."

"What kind of punishment?" she asked in alarm.

"I prefer spankings."

"Oh my…" she exclaimed, a blush coloring her cheeks. He felt her tremble in his arms, and smiled to himself.

He knew for a kindred spirit like Autumn, who desired to please, punishments would be few and far between. However, the knowledge they might happen would keep her constantly on her toes.

Tono tightened his grip around her throat and leaned in to kiss her as he slowly poured wax over her left nipple. She stayed still but moaned as he kissed her, sending fire to his loins. He took his time, slowly covering her chest in wax while he lost himself in her kisses.

When he could no longer take the sexual tension, Tono blew out the candle and set it on the floor. He lifted her from him to scoot beside her.

Tono stared at her swollen pussy and stated, "Next time the wax will caress a more sensitive area."

Autumn gasped.

While she imagined that scene, Tono removed the pin and took off her prosthetic. He felt her tense when he rolled off the liner, but she made no attempt to stop him.

Once Autumn was completely naked, he opened his kimono, exposing his raging hard-on to her.

"This is what you do to me."

She grinned, obviously pleased to see his state of arousal.

"Our challenge is to see if we can remove all of this wax with our spirited lovemaking," he informed her.

"Oh, that's a challenge I wholeheartedly support, dear Master."

Tono was touched by her spontaneous endearment and leaned over to kiss her before settling between her legs. "Show me your garden that's bursting into life…" He looked down at her wet pussy, admiring its erotic beauty.

Autumn smiled at the reference to the song, and held her breath as she watched him position his cock against her opening. He slowly sank his shaft into her warm depths, groaning with satisfaction as her tight walls embraced him.

She threw her head back, panting in pleasure as they began moving in unison, making the strokes deeper and more pleasurable for them both. With each thrust, Tono purposely rubbed his chest against hers, breaking the wax into pieces.

After several minutes, he stopped and looked down at her. "Are you ready to make wax fly, kohana?"

"*Hai*, Tono," she said, before biting her bottom lip.

Tono increased the tempo of his thrusts, not wanting to scare her with his intensity but desiring to show her the full extent of his passion.

As his strokes became deeper and faster, Autumn's breasts bounced in matching rhythm, causing more and more pieces of red wax to fall away. It was an erotic visual, forcing him to slow down or orgasm at that very moment.

"Don't stop," Autumn begged.

Tono grunted, struggling to maintain control, knowing he didn't have long but spurred on by her plea. He braced himself and commanded gruffly, "Use your safeword if you must, I am about to lose control."

She looked up at him hungrily, at a loss for words.

Tono gritted his teeth in concentration, warning her, "The wax is about to fly."

"Yes!" she moaned fervently.

With no further urging needed, Tono closed his eyes and let his passion loose on her. In the fiery melding of their souls he heard the impassioned cry of Autumn allowing her sensual spirit to finally take over and be free.

Afterward they lay in each other's arms, regaining their breath. He brushed the hair from her face, kissing her sweaty cheek with a sense of profound harmony.

"What are you thinking?" Autumn asked.

"I don't regret a moment of my life, not one second—the positive and the negative—because it led to this."

Destiny had brought Brie Bennett into his life and opened his eyes to what was possible, she in turn had introduced him to Autumn, and now he held his lifemate in his arms. There was no greater gift.

Tono closed his eyes and imagined Brie standing before him, her honey-colored eyes shining with joy, her smile warm and inviting.

Thank you, toriko.

Gratitude filled his heart knowing she was alive and safe...

Rytsar Durov is upset. He sent Tono back home and still must confront Brad Anderson. Bones may be broken.

The Russian Dom intends to take care of Lilly. No one touches *radost moya* and NO ONE hurts his *moye solntse*.

In a world of pain and betrayal, Thane and Brie have brought light into his life. He will do anything to protect them—anything. Find out where that leads in
Her Russian Knight.

COMING NEXT

Her Russian Knight: Brie's Submission

13th Book in the Series

Available Now

Reviews mean the world to me!

I truly appreciate you taking the time to review
Breathe with Me.

If you could leave a review on both Goodreads and the
site where you purchased this eBook from, I would be so
grateful. Sincerely, ~Red

ABOUT THE AUTHOR

Over Two Million readers have enjoyed Red's stories

Red Phoenix – USA Today Bestselling Author
Winner of 8 Readers' Choice Awards

Hey Everyone!

I'm Red Phoenix, an author who also happens to be a submissive in real life. I wrote the Brie's Submission series because I wanted people everywhere to know just how much fun BDSM can be.

There is a huge cast of characters who are part of Brie's journey. The further you read into the story the more you learn about each one. I hope you grow to love Brie and the gang as much as I do.

They've become like family.

When I'm not writing, you can find me online with readers.

I heart my fans! ~Red

To find out more visit my Website

redphoenixauthor.com

Follow Me on BookBub

bookbub.com/authors/red-phoenix

Newsletter: Sign up

redphoenixauthor.com/newsletter-signup

Facebook: AuthorRedPhoenix

Twitter: @redphoenix69

Instagram: RedPhoenixAuthor

I invite you to join my reader Group!

facebook.com/groups/539875076052037

SIGN UP FOR MY NEWSLETTER
HERE FOR THE LATEST RED
PHOENIX UPDATES

FOLLOW ME ON INSTAGRAM
INSTAGRAM.COM/REDPHOENIXAUTHOR

SALES, GIVEAWAYS, NEW RELEAS-
ES, PREORDER LINKS, AND MORE!
SIGN UP HERE
REDPHOENIXAUTHOR.COM/NEWSLETTER-
SIGNUP

Red Phoenix is the author of:

Brie's Submission Series:
Teach Me #1
Love Me #2
Catch Me #3
Try Me #4
Protect Me #5
Hold Me #6
Surprise Me #7
Trust Me #8
Claim Me #9
Enchant Me #10
A Cowboy's Heart #11
Breathe with Me #12
Her Russian Knight #13
Under His Protection #14
Her Russian Returns #15
In Sir's Arms #16
Bound by Love #17
Tied to Hope #18
Hope's First Christmas #19
Secrets of the Heart #20

*You can also purchase the AUDIO BOOK Versions

Also part of the Submissive Training Center world:

Rise of the Dominates Trilogy
Sir's Rise #1
Master's Fate #2
The Russian Reborn #3

Captain's Duet
Safe Haven #1
Destined to Dominate #2

The Russian Unleashed #1

Other Books by Red Phoenix

Blissfully Undone
* Available in eBook and paperback

(Snowy Fun—Two people find themselves snowbound in a cabin where hidden love can flourish, taking one couple on a sensual journey into ménage à trois)

His Scottish Pet: Dom of the Ages
* Available in eBook and paperback

Audio Book: *His Scottish Pet: Dom of the Ages*

(Scottish Dom—A sexy Dom escapes to Scotland in the late 1400s. He encounters a waif who has the potential to free him from his tragic curse)

The Erotic Love Story of Amy and Troy
* Available in eBook and paperback

(Sexual Adventures—True love reigns, but fate continually throws Troy and Amy into the arms of others)

eBooks

Varick: The Reckoning

(Savory Vampire—A dark, sexy vampire story. The hero navigates the dangerous world he has been thrust into with lusty passion and a pure heart)

———————————

Keeper of the Wolf Clan (Keeper of Wolves, #1)

(Sexual Secrets—A virginal werewolf must act as the clan's mysterious Keeper)

———————————

The Keeper Finds Her Mate (Keeper of Wolves, #2)

(Second Chances—A young she-wolf must choose between old ties or new beginnings)

———————————

The Keeper Unites the Alphas (Keeper of Wolves, #3)

(Serious Consequences—The young she-wolf is captured by the rival clan)

———————————

Boxed Set: Keeper of Wolves Series (Books 1-3)

(Surprising Secrets—A secret so shocking it will rock Layla's world. The young she-wolf is put in a position of being able to save her werewolf clan or becoming the reason for its destruction)

Socrates Inspires Cherry to Blossom

(Satisfying Surrender—A mature and curvaceous woman becomes fascinated by an online Dom who has much to teach her)

By the Light of the Scottish Moon

(Saving Love—Two lost souls, the Moon, a werewolf, and a death wish…)

In 9 Days

(Sweet Romance—A young girl falls in love with the new student, nicknamed "the Freak")

9 Days and Counting

(Sacrificial Love—The sequel to *In 9 Days* delves into the emotional reunion of two longtime lovers)

And Then He Saved Me

(Saving Tenderness—When a young girl tries to kill herself, a man of great character intervenes with a love that heals)

Connect with Red on Substance B

Substance B is a platform for independent authors to directly connect with their readers. Please visit Red's Substance B page where you can:

- Sign up for Red's newsletter
- Send a message to Red
- See all platforms where Red's books are sold

Visit Substance B today to learn more about your favorite independent authors.

Made in USA - Kendallville, IN
1169190_9780692815120
09.23.2020 0906